THE HOUSE IN THE PINES

THE HOUSE IN THE PINES

Margaret Carr

CHIVERS

British Library Cataloguing in Publication Data available

This Large Print edition published by BBC Audiobooks Ltd, Bath, 2009.
Published by arrangement with the Author.

U.K. Hardcover ISBN 978 1 408 44140 4
U.K. Softcover   ISBN 978 1 408 44141 1

Printed and bound in Great Britain by
CPI Antony Rowe, Chippenham and Eastbourne

CHAPTER ONE

Lynn Raynor collected her hired car from de Gando airport on the island of Gran Canaria and pulled out into the afternoon traffic. It was her first holiday abroad in three years and she meant to enjoy herself.

She drove with care, adjusting to driving on the right hand side of the road as she passed under the flyover and curved up on to the south-bound motorway. She pulled in behind a dark blue Jaguar and settled back knowing she was now on a direct route to Playa Del Ingles.

When the blue car in front of her braked suddenly she couldn't avoid hitting it with a bang. The shock reverberated down her nervous system. She had barely recovered when she caught sight of a tall, dark man thrusting himself out of the Jaguar, an aura of anger surrounding him as he marched towards her.

A spate of Spanish lashed down through her open window until he realised she wasn't understanding a word he said.

'Tourist,' he spat out like a bad taste from his mouth. 'Are you hurt?' he continued in perfect English.

She shook her head, then finding her voice said, 'No thanks to you,' seeing attack as the better part of valour. 'Why on earth did you

1

brake like that? I didn't stand a chance.'

'If you'd been paying attention you would have braked as well when that car tried to pull in between myself and the wagon in front of me. Why do you people hire cars once a year when in all probability you don't even own one at home? Then you come out here and treat it as some kind of practice circuit!'

He left the window to take a look at the damage. Lynn was furious at his accusation.

'For your information,' she said, climbing out of the car and following him round to where the crumpled nose of her little Ford was embedded in the Jaguar's boot, 'I own a car and a ten-year clean driving licence.'

In reality she was horrified at the seeming damage her run-in with the bigger car had done. She heard him say something in Spanish that she was sure was rude as he climbed back into his car and eased it forward to make sure the two cars would separate without further damage. There was a tearing, grinding sound as the cars came apart.

Lynn's heart skipped a beat as she chewed on her lower lip. She was so angry she felt like kicking his car.

'You'll have to contact your car-hire company as soon as you reach your destination,' he said in a patronising tone, as though he was speaking to an idiot.

'I'll make sure they know it was your fault.'

'Fault doesn't come into it. You hit me and

if I were you I'd drive a little more carefully in future. You're not in England now.'

Muttering viciously, she turned her back on him and climbed into the driving seat of the Ford praying that the bump would not have affected its running ability. He stood aside as she turned the key. A loud, dry wail came from the engine.

It stuttered once or twice and died. She repeated the procedure several more times with the same results. Then the door was jerked open and in a weary voice he said one word.

'Out.'

The traffic was tearing by them in the outside lane when a police car pulled on to the hard shoulder and drew up. Lynn's insides started to play up all over again. Now she was glad that she had bumped into a local and not another tourist, and by the look of it, she thought, an influential local.

The policeman greeted the stranger with a salute and they conversed in rapid Spanish, totally ignoring her.

And that's the way I like it, Lynn thought, keeping a low profile.

The policeman glanced towards her a couple of times and she concluded that they were talking about her but he didn't approach her. With a shrug he helped the stranger to jerk the bonnet of the car free and after a few adjustments the policeman turned the key in

3

the ignition and the engine turned over with a cough.

Lynn rushed over and climbed into the driving seat as the policeman strode back to his car.

'Thank you for your help,' she mumbled to the stranger, before clipping on her seat belt and pushing the car into gear.

He gave a brisk nod and headed back to his own car. He kept tucked in behind her all the way to Playa Del Ingles then disappeared in amongst the town's traffic.

Lynn found her apartment without any bother by following the instructions given to her by the holiday company. She parked in a nearby street after depositing her luggage in reception, then walked back, picked up her key and took the lift up to the second floor. In the apartment there was a twin bedroom, shower room and small kitchen at the end of the lounge, with two gas rings, a sink, a fridge and a row of cupboards all hidden behind louvre doors. Her balcony looked out over the street. The apartment was clean and the soft furnishings crisp and bright and she was well pleased with it.

She smiled as she dumped her cases on one of the beds and lay back on the other. Despite the bad start and that awful man she just knew she was going to have a wonderful time here.

CHAPTER TWO

Two days later, Lynn sighed as the warm air caressed her bare shoulders. Her body was still adjusting to the change in temperature after the bitter cold of a North of England winter.

The warm March sun of the Canaries was as close to paradise as anyone could wish, she thought. The hire company had replaced her car, and her insurance had covered it. The world was on an even keel once more.

On the street below her balcony, a tour bus disgorged its consignment of new visitors to the island. Cases were being piled in a haphazard fashion on to the pavement as tired, pale-skinned people circled and weaved in an attempt to claim their property.

Some were making their way in straggled formation across the road to an apartment block on the other side when an open-topped Jeep full of young people swung around the corner and ploughed straight into the baggage-carrying tourists.

Lynn's mouth fell open with shock then she was pushing her feet into sandals and grabbing a T-shirt as she ran from the room. Down two flights of stairs, she emerged on to the walkway that skirted the swimming pool. Once on to the pavement, she pushed her way through the gathering crowd and kneeled down by the first person she found on the ground.

It was an elderly gentleman holding a clean handkerchief someone had given him to his head. Lynn eased his hand away and saw that, although there was some heavy bleeding, it was only superficial. His hands were grazed but he smiled stoically and tried to get up. Other people had helped him to his feet as Lynn moved on.

One quick-thinking person was standing in the centre of the road directing traffic away from the accident as police horns sounded in the distance. The luggage had taken the brunt of the damage, she noticed, as she glanced across the burst cases and scattered belongings.

A middle-aged woman and two children were crying, a young woman had skinned knees and a man trying to gather together his belongings looked to have a broken collar bone that someone had temporarily strapped up with a scarf.

Five of the young people from the Jeep were attempting to right it from its upside down position when Lynn spotted the tip of a brown sandal protruding from beneath the rear of the vehicle.

'Stop, that's the wrong thing to do,' she shouted.

There was some confusion until they understood what she wanted then they stopped rocking the Jeep and made way for Lynn. By now the police had arrived and were pushing the crowd back. A voice spoke in Spanish at Lynn's shoulder, but she ignored it and pointed to the sandal beneath the Jeep.

A great deal of talking broke out and the Jeep was gently raised up lifting the weight from the rear. Lynn was down on the ground before anyone could object, wriggling beneath the upturned vehicle.

The sandal led to a leg encased in denim, a yellow T-shirt, then a face of white marble and a thatch of dusty blonde hair. The foot and leg were intact, the face and head unmarked. The nearest arm was uninjured when she checked it but the other was out-flung and the hand pinned beneath a wedge of seating.

The far leg was definitely broken in at least two places to be at the angle it was. What concerned Lynn most was the trickle of blood seeping from his right ear. Gently she turned his head to the right to allow the ear to drain. Someone was shouting to her from beyond the vehicle and she struggled backward after reassuring the unconscious boy and deciding she could do no more.

The receptionist from Lynn's apartments had explained to the police that Lynn was a nurse and as she straightened, a doctor was talking to her in English. She explained what she had seen of the patient's injuries and this enabled the doctor to instruct the police on

7

the best way to remove the Jeep. In no time the road was cleared and the young man on his way to hospital in the ambulance, siren screaming.

Only the police remained, taking the names and addresses of those involved. Lynn tried to slip back to her apartment unobserved but was delayed by the doctor's praise to the police of her quick thinking, which in turn led to more questioning.

Now, as she stood behind the open doors of her balcony and gazed down at the street, it was as though nothing had ever happened there. She stood for a few minutes longer watching the people going about their business, then turned back into the apartment and put a pan of water on the gas ring to boil. There were never any kettles in holiday accommodation and Lynn, like all good English people, was in need of a cup of tea.

This holiday was, as much as a well-earned rest, by way of compensation for the job she had lost due to cut-backs. There had been a post for her in the new set-up, but she had turned it down on principle. She sighed over her cup of tea.

Why, she asked herself, should she take on more stress and responsibility for no more money, when hospital managers were being paid large bonuses for no more work than they were doing now? When her two weeks holiday was up, she would go home and turn a new leaf. She loved her profession but there was still time to change direction.

*   *   *

Returning from an afternoon on the beach the following day, Lynn noticed a dark blue Jaguar parked against the kerb outside her apartment block. A man in a chauffeur's uniform was leaning against the bonnet, idly thumbing through the pages of a notebook. As Lynn turned down the short flight of stairs to the reception area she saw the girl at the desk signal someone beyond Lynn's shoulder. Immediately the man in the uniform was standing in front of her.

'Excuse, please, but you are Miss Raynor?'

'Yes.'

'I am told to ask if you wish to visit the hospital.'

Lynn frowned.

'Hospital?'

'Si, to visit the son of my employer, Senor Falcon. The young man you rescued yesterday, did you not? His father now wishes to show his gratitude to you.'

Lynn eyed the familiar car with exasperation. Please, she prayed, not him again.

'But I didn't rescue his son. I simply assessed his injuries.'

'Do you not then wish to see him?'

9

'Well, yes, I would like to know how he is, but I'm in no fit state to go visiting at the moment.'

She swept a hand down the front of her sun top and cut-off shorts.

'Ah, no problem. I will wait.'

Lynn shrugged and continued on up the stairs to her apartment. As she showered, she toyed with the idea of asking about the possibilities of work here on the island.

The hospital would be a good place to ask. There would be legalities to be got through of course but it wouldn't hurt to find out. She imagined living here all year round and, flushed by her inspiration, she dressed carefully in a blue print dress and soft white sandals. Adding a touch of pink lipstick, she picked up a small clutch purse and a white sweater in case it grew chilly when the sun went down.

The driver explained that the boy had spent the previous night in the nearby hospital of San Augustin but then that morning he had been moved to Las Palmas to be closer to his family.

It took nearly an hour to drive to the hospital in Las Palmas, the capital. The car drew to a stop at the main entrance and the driver left the car to escort her to the chief nurse.

Lynn was shown into a deeply-carpeted room with soft chairs and low tables. Lamps

10

and magazines were placed strategically around the room. It looked more like a department store window display than a hospital waiting-room. The grey-suited man staring out of the window turned at her entrance and Lynn felt a hysterical giggle run up her throat as she recognised the man she had bumped into on the road the day she'd arrived.

'Miss Raynor, thank you for coming,' he said without a show of recognition.

Her hand disappeared into his and she swallowed hard. He towered over her, big, lean and strong, like the grip in which he still held her hand. She remembered his hands and funnily enough his ears. They were the first things she noticed about a person and what they told her rarely let her down. His hands were perfect—long, slim hands with short, clean nails, firm, not podgy. He had generous ears, large without sticking out, no fleshy lobes or thick rims but curved smoothly to the sides of his head. His dark hair was clipped neatly at collar length.

Cool grey eyes with thick dark lashes washed over her then came back to study her face and with a small gasp of surprise Lynn realised the attraction was mutual.

Suddenly conscious that she was staring Lynn lowered her gaze and moved back a pace.

'How is—er—your son?'

'His name is Peter. His leg is broken in two places, as you surmised, and his left hand has some tendon damage but it was the head injury that worried us. However I have been told that he will live and for that we must be thankful.'

He turned away from her and made to sit down, then checked himself.

'The name is Falcon, by the way, Luis Falcon. Please be seated. The doctors will be finished with Peter directly then we may see him for a short while.'

Lynn moved to another chair and sat down. Her legs had a decided wobble from the surge of her emotions. He was so like everything she had ever dreamed of in a man, from his looks to the deep, strong timbre of his voice, yet he'd said nothing about their earlier meeting and she doubted he even remembered her.

The door opened and a tall, thin woman came into the room. Her suit was silk, her perfume wafting in a breeze behind her. Not a single hair was out of place on her beautiful dark head, nor a wrinkle marring the perfection of her finely-boned face, yet Lynn thought a certain hardness of expression spoiled the woman's over-all good looks.

Luis Falcon rose to his feet once more.

'Sofia,' he said, addressing the new arrival, 'this is Miss Raynor, the young woman who helped save Peter. Miss Raynor,' he said, turning to Lynn, 'my mother-in-law's niece,

Sofia Mateo de Sosa.'

Lynn held out her hand.

'Senora.'

The woman's hand brushed with a feather-like touch across Lynn's own. 'Miss Raynor.'

Her voice was brittle and negative, making Lynn feel invisible.

Senora de Sosa picked up a magazine, sat down and flicked through its pages. Lynn glanced from one to the other several times. What strange people, she thought. Where were the hugs and kisses, the expressions of concern for the patient that she knew her own family would have given amongst each other?

After several silent minutes had elapsed Lynn said, 'I think I'll come back tomorrow. I don't want to intrude on your visit.'

The man's eyebrows rose a fraction.

'You can't wait? You have another appointment perhaps?'

'No, but I doubt your son will be fit enough to see strangers even supposing the doctors will let me in.'

He rose to his feet along with her. The senora didn't look up from her magazine.

'I'm sorry you can't stay. Peter will want to thank you,' he said.

Lynn smiled politely though she doubted very much that Peter would be in any fit state to thank her or otherwise.

Falcon's eyes searched her face and Lynn wondered if he was trying to place where he had seen her. Then she was out of the room and hurrying towards the exit.

At the central desk she stopped for an update on Peter's condition. Glad to hear he was in no immediate danger, she went on to ask about the possibilities of work.

The young nurse shrugged her shoulders and tried to explain how to apply for work, while writing down an address for Lynn to seek out.

'The people here will help you,' the nurse said with a smile, handing over the piece of paper.

Probably the equivalent of an employment office, Lynn whispered to herself as she left the building.

A voice close behind her made her jump.

'It's the address of a nursing agency.'

Lynn's heart gave a great bump before racing twice as fast as it should. 'Senor?' was all she could think of saying.

'With you leaving so suddenly, I omitted to offer you the use of the car to take you home. If you can tell me what time you wish to visit my son tomorrow, I will send the car for you again.'

'Oh, no, please. I'll find my own way here.'

His face stiffened as though she had insulted him.

'You are on holiday. It is not to be expected that you should spend your allowance travelling to see my son.'

Sensing the strong pride in this man, Lynn made a frantic effort to back pedal.

'Well, thank you, that's very kind of you. Shall we say two o'clock?' she said apologetically.

A quiver of a smile tugged one corner of his mouth as he offered his hand.

'Buenas tardes, Miss Raynor. I look forward to seeing you again,' he said, with a slight nod of his head.

Lynn sat in the back of the car hardly daring to breath. Would he be there tomorrow and if he was, she scolded herself, what difference is it to you? He's a married man with a teenage son.

CHAPTER THREE

To Lynn's disappointment, there was no sign of the boy's father at the hospital the following afternoon. But she was to be allowed to meet the young man she had helped.

'Senor Falcon insisted that you be treated as one of the family,' the nurse confided to Lynn.

They were walking down a white corridor with blue doors on either side in this the private wing of the hospital. Her own soft sandals and the nurse's rubber-soled shoes made a squeaky sigh on the highly-polished floor. Smells of antiseptics invaded the air sending Lynn's professional emotions into overdrive.

'There was no brain damage?' she asked the nurse.

'No. He has had a scan which was clear. He has pain naturally but the doctor expects a complete recovery.'

'His hand?'

'They operated. The tendon damage was minimal.'

The nurse opened a door on the right saying to the occupant as they entered, 'I have brought you Miss Raynor, the lady your father told you about, Peter.'

Lynn smiled at the young man in the bed.

'Great, you're young and pretty, what a

16

relief. The way my father described you I was afraid you might be some old dragon,' he said, smiling cheekily.

That hurt! She would have liked to have known exactly how his father had described her.

'Hello,' she said, walking towards the bed with her hand extended. 'My name is Rosalind, but my friends call me Lynn.'

'Hi, Lynn. My father tells me I owe you my life.'

'That's a slight exaggeration.'

'It suits me fine. I don't mind owing you my life.'

She caught the twinkle in his warm brown eyes and thought how disgustingly beautiful he was, for a man. His shoulder-length blonde hair had been bleached nearly white by the sun and curled around an oval face with neat bones and a straight nose. His bow-shaped mouth was smiling at her now. An infectious laugh escaped them both as they accepted each other's scrutiny.

'I didn't know what to bring you,' Lynn said, producing several magazines covering topics as diverse as computers and cycling.

'Stay, please,' he said. 'The most comfortable chair is that one in the corner. It must be. It's the one Sofia sat in earlier and she's renowned for grabbing the best of everything.'

Lynn pulled a wry smile as she thought of

17

the cool woman she had met in the waiting-room the previous afternoon.

'Well, I'll stay for a short while perhaps.'

'My father is not expected today. But Sofia will be back tonight.'

'Your English is excellent.'

Peter laughed.

'My grandfather was English and my father was determined that I be bilingual. Grandmother Medina does not like it but my father's word is law so she has to put up with it.'

'What does your mother think?'

His face sobered momentarily.

'My mother died when I was seven.'

Lynn's soft heart collided with her curiosity.

'I'm sorry.'

'Are you staying near the scene of the crash?'

'Yes, it happened just outside my apartments, the Flamingo Apartments.'

'Ah, yes,' he said, grimacing as a movement in bed caused him pain. 'My father must remove you to one of our best hotels. A suite with a sea view. How much of your holiday is left?'

'Hey, just a minute,' Lynn cried, holding up her hands in mock horror. 'There's no way I can afford any first-class hotels even if I was on the point of departure. As it is I have only just arrived.'

'Please,' he went on, trying to pull himself

up in the bed. 'Do not insult us. No-one is suggesting for a moment that you pay. It beholds us to repay you for your kindness.'

'This is getting out of hand, Peter. I came today only to check that you were going to recover. Nobody owes anybody anything. Now, I'll be on my way. Good to have met you,' she said, rising from the chair and preparing to leave.

'On this island we do not abandon someone who has saved our life. My father will be in touch. Hasta la vista, Lynn.'

Lynn was counting out her foreign currency next morning when she heard a sharp rap on an apartment door. She stopped what she was doing and waited for it to be repeated, not quite sure that it was her door. It came again and while unable to imagine who might be calling on her, she answered it. He stood there, looking totally out of place.

'Miss Raynor, I wondered if you could spare me a few moments of your time.'

Lynn, puzzled as to what he might have to say, opened the door wider and allowed him to enter.

'How can I help you, Senor Falcon?'

'My son tells me you do not wish to acknowledge our gratitude.' Lynn felt the sting of an embarrassed blush rise to her face.

'I don't mean to be rude, but . . . '

'Do you still wish to work on the island, Miss Raynor?'

'I was thinking about it, yes.'

'Would you consider private nursing?' he asked, casting a casual glance around her accommodation. 'An elderly lady with angina and arthritis and a young man recovering from injury.'

'My experience is in hospital work.'

'But you would consider it?' he persisted.

Lynn was on the point of turning him down, when he mentioned the figure on offer.

'This could be paid into a local bank, plus your own car and rooms, of course.'

Lynn suddenly felt as if she had been smacked in the face, such was her surprise.

'We are talking about my working for you, aren't we?'

With raised eyebrows he asked, 'Have you a problem with that?'

'Not exactly, no. It's, well, after talking to your son yesterday, I wondered if you were inventing this job for me.'

'What did my son say to make you think that? My mother-in-law is seventy-two and in need of constant attention which her niece cannot give her full time. Your work will make the burden easier for her. Peter may only need your attention for the next few weeks once he is home. Whether you decide to stay on after my son is on his feet again or use the time to find alternative employment is up to you. If you need time to think it over please let me know no later than tomorrow afternoon.'

When he had gone, Lynn slumped down on to the settee and stared at the print on the opposite wall. Well, my girl, you have got yourself a job after all, she thought, and what a job.

The accommodation was bound to be first class if he could afford to offer a salary like the one he had just offered her. Her own car, and the work didn't sound too onerous. Of course on the down side, she would lose what was left of her holiday, but the time off was generous, supposing she could get them pinned down to sticking to it. One of the hazards of private nursing, she knew, was the inability of employers to accept the off-duty times stated in their contracts.

She glanced at the small, printed business card he had given her and read Luis Falcon, Director of Canteras (import/export) Co., Ltd., and the telephone number beneath. She chewed on her lip for a while, debating the wisdom of what she was about to do.

The following morning, after ringing Luis Falcon and accepting the job, she sat on her balcony enjoying a lunch of fresh rolls, ham, cheese and orange juice. She thought about the changes she would have to make to the life she had left behind her. Her parents would need to be told and friends contacted if she was to ask them to put her belongings into storage.

She would write to the landlord of her two-bedroom flat. The lease was six monthly with a month's notice either way. Her deposit would cover that. She reminded herself of the cold, rain-washed streets and the dark passage and stairs that led up to her flat and shuddered. She would ring her parents regularly and visit when she could afford it but apart from that she would be committing herself to a life on her own on Gran Canaria.

CHAPTER FOUR

The Casa Mariana stood facing a small, cobbled square in the Vegueta district of Las Palmas. Its tall, stone frontage looked forbidding with its heavy, carved door, shuttered windows and empty balconies. The chauffeur rang a great metal bell by the door and as Lynn climbed from the car, a small, bent man came out of the house and collected the cases the chauffeur deposited on the ground.

'Senorita, please to come this way,' an equally small, dark woman said as she appeared in the doorway. 'My name is Ana. I am the housekeeper of Senora Medina.'

So, Lynn thought, it's the house of the senora, not Luis Falcon. Does that mean I'm an employee of the old lady and not her son-in-law?

'The senoras await you in the sala,' the housekeeper informed her.

Lynn followed Ana through a large, stone-floored hallway whose iron wall sconces and heavy furniture gave it a mediaeval look. They crossed an open-air courtyard with a central fountain and turned up a wide, carpeted, stone staircase and along a landing dark with the life-sized portraits of the long dead.

All rather spooky, Lynn decided.

The room she was shown into was wide and long, its three windows heavily swathed in lace and damask. Beautifully-carved cabinets stood along two of the white walls armed by heavy, straight-backed chairs with wooden arms and seats that looked as though they had never been sat in since the occupants had worn chain mail! A variety of small chairs and tables were arranged around the room.

'Miss Raynor, senoras,' Ana announced, before turning and leaving the room.

A pair of beady brown eyes beneath a head of white hair looked up from her embroidery frame.

'Do you speak Spanish?' the older of the two women said in a cold voice.

'I'm afraid not, senora, but I am hoping to learn,' Lynn replied rather hesitantly.

She was aware of the other younger woman in the room who had yet to speak. She held a glass of something in her hand and was watching her aunt silently.

'Come over here, girl, so I can get a good look at you,' the senora said. Lynn crossed the floor and waited to be invited to sit down, but the small, elderly lady with the ramrod back did no such thing.

Instead she said, 'This is my niece, Senora do Sosa, whom I believe you have already met.'

By now, Lynn was getting the distinct feeling that her presence in their home was not appreciated.

Sofia de Sosa looked her up and down then said, 'In the hospital, I believe.'

Lynn smiled at them, refusing to be daunted by their chilly reception. 'That's right, the night of the accident.'

The senora continued, 'We are a quiet family here. We dislike noise or disturbance in any form. I have arranged for you to sleep in the room next to mine in case I should need you during the night. Any other details I have left to my son-in-law. Please refer to him if you have any enquiries. Ana will show you to your room,' she ended, ringing a small, silver bell on the table by her side.

Ana appeared like magic and Lynn wondered how on earth she had heard the little bell from the ground floor and answered it so promptly. She followed Ana along the balcony that ran above three sides of the courtyard to a room that was dark after the dazzling sun outside.

The walls of her room were white, the floor and furniture a highly-polished dark wood. There was a tall wardrobe, a neat dressing table, a bedside cabinet with a lamp and a water carafe and tumbler next to a comfortable-looking four poster bed. An adjoining small bathroom made her sigh thankfully. Lynn's mood lifted as Ana left telling her that a maid would be up directly to unpack for her.

Lynn had no intention of letting someone else do her unpacking for her and, pulling one of the cases—the old man had left her luggage inside the door—on to the bed, she began to take out her clothes.

'What have you got against the child who will unpack for you? Would you deny her the job?'

Lynn's feet nearly left the floor at the sudden intrusion of Luis Falcon's voice. He stood outlined against the sun in her doorway.

'How long have you been there?' she gasped.

A smile twitched one corner of his mouth.

'The view into the courtyard is preferable to that of the street.' He directed her on to the balcony.

'Beneath us we have Ana's and José's quarters, the kitchens, and laundry.'

He waved down into the open centre of the house.

'There is also a study, office and library. On this floor we have the sala, dining-room, several bedrooms with bathrooms. I have modernised and improved where necessary for comfort and ease but Maria Medina prefers the old ways.'

'It is rather large isn't it, and breath-taking?' she murmured.

'I came to tell you that we eat late here so it may be as well if you were to rest this afternoon and I will see you at six in my office.'

'One moment, senor,' she said as he made to leave her. 'I would like one thing cleared up. Who exactly is my employer, yourself or Senora Medina?'

'I am your employer, Miss Raynor, have no doubt about that.'

CHAPTER FIVE

Later, Lynn wondered whether she was pleased or daunted by Luis Falcon's response. There was a tap on the door and a slim teenager came into the room. She gave Lynn a shy smile and indicated that she was here to unpack Lynn's cases.

Lynn, rather embarrassed by this personal attention, moved out on to the balcony. A deep canopy covered the balcony, sheltering her face from the sun while her arms lay along the warm wood.

When she stepped back into the room several minutes later, she found the maid had finished her work and gone, leaving behind a simple meal of salad and bread on a tray. Lynn was grateful she wouldn't have to join the family for lunch.

Yes, she thought, after enjoying the meal, it would be easy to fall asleep now despite her curiosity about the house and the people in it. She had no intention of taking a siesta but the peacefulness of the house acted like a sedative and, lying down for a rest, she was soon fast asleep.

When she woke, she was at a loss to remember where she was, then as memory returned she noticed that the room was much darker and wondered what time it was. A shiver ran through her as she glanced at her watch. Goodness, it was twenty to five! She had slept the whole afternoon away and she was due in Luis Falcon's office at six o'clock.

A warm shower chased away the remains of her shivers, after which she searched her wardrobe for something suitable to wear. The clothes she had brought with her were, in the main, lightweight cotton and casual. Many changes later she had decided on a pink wrap-around skirt and patterned silk blouse. Her hair she arranged in a knot on top of her head. A touch of pink lipstick and a light brush of mascara and she was ready.

She had mapped out the position of the office in her head, but once down the stairs and on the ground floor she was faced with a series of doors she couldn't place. There was no-one in sight whom she could ask so she opened the first door on the right and peeked in.

It was a library with a central table and straight-backed chairs. The bookshelves were laden with numerous heavy tomes covering three of the four walls while a second table extended along the fourth wall bearing a display of the largest pieces of silver Lynn had ever seen. She couldn't suppress a giggle at the thought of the trouble a burglar might have trying to shift that lot.

The sound of a footstep behind her made her swing round to the courtyard, a flush of guilt on her face. Luis Falcon stood behind her, his expression perplexed.

'Is there someone there?'

'No.'

'I thought I heard you laugh.'

'You did, but it was just to myself.'

Lynn's colour heightened.

'There is something funny about the house?'

'No, not at all,' Lynn rushed to assure him.

He shook his head as though dismissing silly English behaviour.

'I came to show you the way to the office. I thought you might find it confusing at first.'

Lynn fell in beside him and followed him into an extremely modern office with up-to-date technology and walls covered in charts. Fascinated, Lynn stared at an around-the-world time piece, shipping lane charts, old ships, logs and cargo lists from long ago in glass topped cases.

'These are really interesting pieces. Have you been collecting long?' she asked.

'These pieces, Miss Raynor, have been in my family for three centuries,' he replied curtly.

Lynn just stared, then swiftly removed her hand from the case and wiped it down the side of her skirt.

'Your business,' she whispered, 'goes back three centuries?'

He lifted his head and his combined

30

Spanish, English and Canarian heritage blazed from his eyes.

'When you are ready,' he said, indicating a chair to one side of his desk. Lynn sat down.

'I will need to see qualification certificates and at least two testimonials. Do you have business to see to in England before you decide to work here?'

'No, nothing I can't do over the phone.'

'What about family, friends. Do you leave a fiancé, partner or whatever they call it these days?'

Lynn didn't like his tone.

'I only leave my parents and I haven't lived at home for nine years. I shall go back to see them from time to time and,' she said with a smile, 'who knows, they might even come out to see me, though they're not keen on travelling. As for the rest, I don't have a current boyfriend. I'm twenty-eight years old and was engaged to a doctor for four years after which time even I realised he had no intentions of marrying me.'

Her chin jutted forward as she said this for Dr Simon Westfield's treatment of her still rubbed like an unhealed sore. Luis Falcon dropped his head in acknowledgement of her honesty.

When he looked her in the eyes again something had changed. It appeared to Lynn that his glance had softened, but his tone was the same when he spoke.

'My mother-in-law can be difficult. She resents obvious help from strangers. It will take time for her to accept you. While she allows Sofia and Ana to help her dress in the mornings and evenings you will take charge of her medication and see to her needs during the day when Sofia and Ana have other things to do. It will take a while but I'm sure you will cope in time. Peter, on the other hand, should be little bother to you other than trying to monopolise your time. Don't let him. If you have any other problems, you can always find me here when I am at home. Is there anything else you wish to know?'

'Only that we agree on one and a half days off a week.'

'That is understood, of course.'

His attention wandered to some papers on his desk.

'And the senora's hearing? She does have trouble hearing, doesn't she?'

His eyes snapped back to her face.

'Yes, she does. That was very astute of you to notice, but I expected nothing less. Her poor hearing is a definite disadvantage but she is a proud woman and will never admit to it. Now, if there is nothing else, we dine at nine. I will see you then, Miss Raynor.'

She was being dismissed.

Back in her room, Lynn wondered what on earth she was supposed to do now. It was barely seven o'clock. After checking through her clothes to find out where the maid had placed them she wandered into the bathroom to check out her toiletries. She must go shopping now she had decided to stay.

Then she sat down at the dressing-table and wrote to her closest friend, Jean, asking her to send out one or two items that would be of more use to her here than in store in England.

There was a sharp rap on the door just as she licked around the edge of the envelope.

'Come in.'

Luis entered, dressed in a close-fitting black suit with white shirt and red cummerbund and his looks took Lynn's breath away.

'I—er—have no evening wear with me.'

His eyes ran over her from top to toe.

'You look quite respectable as you are. Did no-one inform you that we take drinks in the sala before dinner or do you prefer your own company to ours?'

'I wasn't told.'

'Then you will accompany me now.'

It was more of an order than a question. Lynn put aside her letter and accompanied him along the landing to the room she had first been shown into that morning, the sala. The two ladies of the household merely bent their heads in acknowledgement as Lynn entered the room on Luis' arm. A man of medium height rose from a settee to one side of a tall window. Luis introduced him.

'Miss Raynor, this is my business partner,

33

Enrique Romero. Enrique, Miss Raynor has come to join us as the senora's nurse.'

On a level with herself, Enrique Romero was middle age, overweight and going bald. He stretched out a warm hand and shook hers briefly. His smile was the gentlest she had so far encountered from the adults she'd met and she warmed to him immediately.

'I'm sure Miss Raynor has a Christian name, Luis?'

'Lynn, it's short for Rosalind. My mother is a Shakespearean admirer,' she offered, not waiting for Luis Falcon's recovery for she doubted he remembered her first name anyway.

'That's a pretty name. So you are a nurse, a worthwhile occupation, I'm sure. I hope you will stay here in Gran Canaria for some time to come.' Lynn smiled, and thanked him.

*   *   *

For the first few days, the evening meal was too much for her as she tended to retire immediately afterwards. But by the fourth evening she had developed enough confidence to stay longer.

Sofia and her mother played cards most evenings and Luis, with Enrique when he called, invariably disappeared into the office leaving Lynn to her own devices. She would bring down a book and read or write a letter until she was tired enough to go to bed.

On the odd occasion that Luis did not retire to the office he and Lynn would make up a foursome with the senora and her niece. Lynn had noticed earlier how possessive Sofia became when in the presence of Luis, so it came as no surprise when she demanded him as her playing partner.

'My aunt and I play so often that I am aware of every move she will make,' she said to Lynn with a fixed smile. 'A change of partner is a challenge, is it not, Luis?'

Her smile changed to one of a cat anticipating cream, and Lynn wondered what kind of relationship these two shared. Luis' only response was to raise his eyebrows and lay down the first card. Lynn was left to partner the senora.

'Think, girl, before you play your hand. Have you never played before? What a slow brain you have. I hope you manage my medication better than you do these cards,' the old woman said, making no attempt to hide her slight annoyance.

The games became a nightmare for Lynn. If it wasn't the Senora Medina carping on at her lack of skill it was Sofia remarking on her lack of dress sense or offering unwanted advice on make-up or deportment, always showing Lynn at a disadvantage, while under the disguise of being helpful. What really upset Lynn was that Luis paid no attention to these catty remarks from his family, when he must have realised how distressing they were for her.

When she entered the sala that evening after dinner and saw the card table set for four she gave an inward groan. As they went to be seated Luis moved round until he was opposite Lynn.

'A change of partners, I think.'

Sofia could not hide her disapproval.

'We were successful, you and I, natural partners. I can't imagine why you want to change now, but you are right.'

She shrugged her shoulders.

'We must give the underdogs a try.'

Maria Medina gave her niece a sharp look but said nothing.

CHAPTER SIX

Two hours later it was a different story. As she grumbled incessantly in Spanish, Sofia, with thinned lips and flared nostrils, tossed her cards on the table and announced she was tired and going to bed.

Luis rose also and offered the women a nightcap then snapped at them in their own language as they exchanged words with each other and rang the bell for Ana to help the senora to bed. When the door had closed behind them he turned back to Lynn.

'Sofia and the senora are upset because we won,' he said, a smile curving his lips.

Then his eyes fell to Lynn's face and the smile gave way to a frown. Lynn's hand was unsteady as she took a last gulp of her sherry and placed the glass down on the nearest table. Why did these women hate her so much? What had she done to them? She was used to personality clashes with patients and colleagues alike in hospital where you just had to deal with them as best you could, but never before had she come across such open hostility as she had read in Senora Medina's eyes tonight.

A hand under her chin threw her head backward until she was gazing into a pair of steel grey eyes.

'You are not going to tell me that you are afraid of an old woman, are you?'

She felt his eyes boring into her mind and stepped back out of reach.

'Of course not. I'm trying to understand how you managed to win with such a handicap of a partner.'

The smile flitted across his face once more, lifting a corner of his mouth, but his eyes never lost contact with her.

'Good-night, Rosalind Raynor,' he said as she left the room.

Three days later, Peter came home with his hand in a bandage and strapped to his chest by a sling. The broken leg was plastered from hip to toes and protruded from his wheelchair like a battering ram. The old man, José, pushed him into the sala that evening.

'Hi, Lynn, I knew I would see you again.'

He pushed away from the old man guiding the chair with one hand and whizzed a wobbly course to Lynn's side.

'Peter,' Luis' voice rapped out, 'your grandmother and aunt are waiting to greet you.'

Peter winked up at Lynn then allowed José to push him across to the other side of the room where his female relatives waited for his attention with cool acceptance. They spoke in fluent Spanish as José withdrew and Luis asked Lynn what she would like to drink.

When Luis returned with her drink, Enrique

had arrived and excused himself to welcome Peter home. Luis turned back to Lynn.

'We had better all be on first-name terms. It will save confusion that way. All except my mother-in-law, of course. I don't believe she would appreciate it,' he added.

He sounded as though he begrudged her the familiarity, Lynn thought, but when she looked up at him she realised he was saying it tongue in cheek. She smiled and a short while later they moved in to dinner. The senora still hadn't forgiven Lynn for winning at cards on the previous two evenings, not eating with the staff, nor for being allocated a guest room instead of the cubby hole adjoining her own suite. She made her disapproval of Lynn's position obvious in a number of ways, one of which was to complain that there wasn't enough work to justify Lynn staying.

Although Lynn was meant to ease the burden of responsibility from the shoulders of Sofia and Ana this had proved to be an extremely difficult task as the elderly woman refused point blank to allow her to do anything for her other than to hand out her medication and do a little fetching and carrying.

Certainly not what she had been trained for, Lynn angrily admitted to herself.

*   *   *

Now Peter was home, she concentrated

instead on helping him to fill his time as usefully as possible while waiting for his leg to heal.

Lynn sat in the courtyard, the sun hot on her shirt-covered back, listening to the tinkle of the fountain. Peter would arrive any minute urging her to join him in a board game or longing to release some pent-up fury at one of the members of the family. But for now she lay back and enjoyed the peace.

She had been with the family a month now and try as she might she was still no further forward in her attempted friendship with Sofia. Every time she thought she was near a breakthrough, the indomitable senora closed the breech. The old lady's complaints had increased over the past week, too. Lynn was rude, she said, untrustworthy, spied on the family's private matters, the list was never ending according to her.

'Lynn, catch these for me, please.'

Peter hobbled out into the courtyard, papers clutched between his crutch and his side as he tried to manoeuvre himself along without losing the sliding documents.

Lynn leaped to her feet and snatched the papers minutes before they would have fluttered to the ground. Setting them on the wall that surrounded the fountain she turned back to help Peter settle himself into one of the cane chairs that stood around a small table.

40

'What's it to be today then?' she asked, placing his papers before him.

'I want you to look at these brochures and tell me what you think.' Eagerness shone from his eyes as he pushed the material over to her.

'But I can't read Spanish.'

Lynn gave him a searching look as she picked up the glossy-backed books. They were brochures for a North London art college. Several pamphlets and leaflets introduced various alternatives to the courses described in the brochure.

'I didn't know you were thinking of going to an English college.'

'I have been thinking about it for some time now. I needed to be certain that Art and Design was what I wanted to do. The family will not be pleased. I must be very determined.'

He stretched across the table towards her.

'My father agrees that I may continue my education in England but he and Enrique want me to concentrate on business studies, but sometimes my head explodes with colour, my hands twist with the need to shape images of perfection, images that say something, that give messages to people.'

'Have you tried to explain this to your father?' Lynn asked, withdrawing her hand from his.

'Several times but he and Enrique see only my entering the business with them.'

41

His eyes clouded over and his mouth thinned, reminding Lynn of his likeness to his father.

'They cannot see that my art could benefit them also, only in a different way. My father says there will be opportunities to paint in my free time, but I do not want to paint as a child paints, Lynn. I want to create, to influence people. I need freedom and colour.'

'Well, you won't get much colour in England,' Lynn said with a grin, 'not in the winter anyway. But, yes, I do know what you mean. What is it you want from me?'

'I want you to speak for me.'

He smiled, his eyes once more shining with suppressed excitement. 'To the family.'

'You are joking, I hope,' she exclaimed in disbelief.

'No, I don't joke. You are older, you come from London, they will listen to you because you have experience of these things.'

'I know nothing of commercial art, Peter.'

'Please, Lynn, tell them this is a good college. That I will have much influence from attending this college.'

Lynn groaned inwardly.

'Peter, you know I'm not popular with your family. Why would they listen to me about such an important matter as your future? I'm an outsider.'

She was thumbing through the brochure as Peter said, 'You won't help me then?'

'Of course I'll help, any way I can, but believe me it won't benefit your cause to have me speak to your family.'

'I know how difficult grandmother and Sofia are making your life here. They are very foolish people. It is because you are getting in the way of their plans?'

'Plans?'

'Si, I know how they work. Grandmother has decided that Sofia and my father should marry but my father looks upon you with favour and they don't like it.'

He made a face and shrugged his shoulders. Lynn felt the hot blood run up her neck and set her face aflame.

'Peter, I'm sure they think no such thing.'

'So you see it would be a waste of time to speak to them but if you were to speak to my father.' He paused. 'Please, Lynn, he might listen to you and I could speak to my grandmother. I'm sure I can persuade her you are no threat to her plans.'

Lynn's face had paled and grown strangely still.

'Well, I'll be very grateful if you can intercede with your grandmother and I will try to talk to your father but I can't promise that it will make any difference. In all probability, I'll be told to mind my own business.'

CHAPTER SEVEN

Luis wasn't alone in the office after dinner the following evening when she knocked on the door. Enrique was there, bending over the fax machine.

'I think you should know,' Luis said, after indicating that she should be seated, 'that my mother-in-law has informed us that you have been encouraging Peter in his wish to study art at college.'

Lynn was shocked. She hadn't had time to broach the subject with them let alone be accused of encouraging Peter to do anything. When Luis had suggested at dinner that she should join him in the office later she'd hoped she would get the opportunity to speak to him on Peter's behalf, never dreaming for a minute that Peter himself may have already taken matters into his own hands and mentioned her name.

'We are aware of Peter's ambition but feel it concerns no-one but his family,' Enrique spoke gently.

Lynn took a deep breath, aware of Luis' eyes boring through her, hoping to find evidence of some evil intent, no doubt.

'I don't know what the senora has said, but all I have done is promise Peter I'd speak to you about his ambitions for the future. I've not encouraged him in any way, in any kind of disobedience. Why, anybody with two eyes in their head can see he needs no encouragement. His desperate enthusiasm for this art course is written all over his face.'

'Nevertheless, I have endorsed the family's view that Peter will be better served by committing to a business course first. If he makes a success of that then will be the time to consider further education,' Luis said.

Lynn could feel anger swelling inside her. They obviously had no idea how Peter felt. Had he ever been allowed to talk to them the way he had talked to her the previous day? Were they deaf to the excitement that entered his voice when he spoke of art? She glanced across at Enrique then back to Luis whose brows lifted, daring her to question his authority.

'I'm amazed a family can be so blind to one of its member's needs. But then,' she said, rising to her feet, 'nothing in this job surprises me.'

'I haven't dismissed you, Miss Raynor.'

Enrique made a tutting sound and said, 'You must understand, Lynn, family values are very strong here in Canaria. Oh, I know we are a cosmopolitan island and the young people very fashionable and free thinking. But the older members of a family can often see beyond the enthusiasms of youth. In a good family, youth depends upon the experiences

45

and knowledge of its older members.'

His eyes moved to the stone-faced Luis.

'As head of the family, Luis has taken everyone's feelings into account and made a decision. It is now up to every member of that family to obey his ruling.'

'Isn't that rather outdated? I don't believe for a minute Senor Falcon has taken Peter's feelings into account. If he had, he would be in no doubt as to the strength of those feelings, or the pain that going against them may cause.'

'So,' Luis Falcon snapped, 'you admit to encouraging him to disobey me.'

'I admit nothing.'

'But you think you know better what's best for my son than I do.'

'No, yes, I just know you are wrong not to listen to him.'

Enrique clasped his hands and turned to face the wall. A grim-faced Luis gave her permission to go but not until he warned her.

'I forbid you to discuss this subject with Peter again. If you do I shall have to ask you to leave my employ.'

Lynn stood outside the office door trying hard not to fling it open and tell him to stuff his job. After a while she calmed down and crossed the courtyard to the staircase. Now she was wishing she had never taken the job in the first place.

Peter was lying in wait for her at the top of the stairs.

'I saw you disappear with Father and wondered if you would take the chance to speak to him.'

Lynn frowned at him as they turned along the balcony towards her room. 'Are you saying you haven't spoken to anyone about your college?' she asked.

'Of course not. I am waiting for you to speak to my father first.' Lynn stopped by her door and swung round to face Peter.

'Then I think you should know that I have just been told off for encouraging you in your ambitions to study art. Apparently someone told your grandmother, who lost no time in informing Enrique and your father.'

The look of annoyance on Peter's face was familiar to Lynn and she didn't have to look far to know why.

'How is this possible?' he asked. 'We spoke to no-one yet it is gossiped throughout the house. I warn you, Lynn, it is that Ana. She spies for grandmother. Her eyes and ears are everywhere. José, he is a good man, you can trust him, but that Ana,' and he slammed his fist on the balustrade. 'What did Father say? Did you plead my case for me?'

Lynn opened the door.

'I did what I could. Now, if you don't mind, I would like to rest.'

Not many days after Lynn's confrontation with Luis over Peter's future, she was told by Sofia that they were to have guests over the weekend and would she please see to the Senora Medina as both herself and Ana would be busy. Lynn nodded her acceptance and hurried off to the senora's rooms. She was surprised at the welcome she received and the total turnabout in the old lady's character.

'Peter tells me you like our island and are looking forward to seeing more of it,' she said in perfect English as she allowed Lynn to help her to bed for the siesta.

'I do indeed, senora,' Lynn replied as she tidied up the room.

'My family owned much land at one time, in the mountains. It is very beautiful up there but then, like all tourists, you would prefer the south. So much more sea and sand, I suppose.'

Lynn got the message, so the change in character was only superficial. 'Not at all, senora. I spent my last half-day in the city and it will take many more before I have seen even half of its wonders.'

A deep silence filled the room and Lynn, without turning back to the woman in the bed, finished her task and left the room. She gave a great sigh of relief to be free of her patient for at least a couple of hours and went off to find out if there was anything she could do to help Sofia and Ana. It was as she was going downstairs that Peter caught up with her, hopping at a terrifying pace with the aid of one crutch.

'Have you heard the news, Lynn? Some

business friends of my father's are coming for the weekend.'

'I know, Sofia told me.'

A frown flashed across his face.

'They do not treat you right, Lynn.'

'Oh, they're trying,' Lynn replied with a slight smile.

'I do not believe Sofia would tell you that the couple who are coming to stay have a beautiful daughter who will make sheep's eyes at my father all the time.'

Lynn laughed at his expression.

'How do you know that?'

'Because I heard Grandmother and Sofia talking about them in the sala. They were furious. Sofia said they could palm her off on to me. But I would not have anything to do with her. She is nearly thirty years old!'

Lynn did a quick reassessment of her own twenty-eight years. 'It strikes me there's more than Ana spying in this house.'

'Ah, but I am the good guy,' Peter said as he hobbled off.

The guests arrived the following morning and the daughter was indeed beautiful, not in the same mould as Sofia but a much softer beauty, one that shone from the inside. Because Hella Coenraad was as intelligent as she was beautiful and could speak several languages, one of them being English, she and Lynn were soon on friendly terms.

Often over the next two days Lynn would

49

look up and catch Luis' eyes upon them while Sofia acted the perfect hostess. It seemed that in her new-found friendship Lynn had also appeased the senora and Sofia by helping to keep their young guest's attentions away from Luis.

On the Sunday evening, all that changed. The guests were due to leave on Monday morning and as a special treat on the Sunday evening Hella was to sing for them. She had a lovely voice which covered every song with perfection.

Enrique sat by Sofia's side and gently touched her arm as Hella's performance came to an end with a rendering of Don't Cry For Me Argentina.

'Enrique has a thing for Sofia but she won't look at him while Father is still available,' Peter whispered into Lynn's ear, as Ana entered the room pushing a trolley from which she began to serve coffee.

Hella left the room to refresh herself. When she returned, her face was a great deal paler and her hand shook as she made her way over to her parents and excused them from the family conversation. As Lynn watched, Hella's mother put a comforting arm around the girl's shoulders while her father crossed swiftly to Luis' side and said something that made his host's jaw clench.

Lynn was on the point of rising and going to see if she could help when Luis snapped out an order that sent Ana hurrying from the room. Lynn crossed to her friend's side.

'Is something wrong? Can I be of any help?'

'My daughter's pendant is missing. It's of great sentimental value to her. It was given to her by her great-grandfather on his death bed,' her mother explained.

'I'm sure it will be found,' Lynn said and tried to comfort her friend. 'It can't have gone far.'

Several minutes passed before Ana returned. She walked straight up to Maria Medina and handed over a small object.

'There, you see it's been found,' Lynn said to Hella.

'Most certainly it has been found, Miss Raynor.'

Sofia's voice, while remaining low key and discreet, nevertheless carried across the full width of the room so that all eyes followed it to Lynn.

'It was found in your room, but then I am sure you have a perfectly good explanation for that. In the meanwhile, Hella, I am sure you are happy to have this returned,' she said crossing to Hella's side and presenting her with the pendant.

With a frown, Lynn slid away from the group surrounding Hella, congratulating her on the finding of her pendant. She closed the door behind her quietly and made her way down the passage, passed the head of the stairs and along to her own room. She was just about to enter when Luis' voice halted her.

'I'll see you downstairs in my office, now.'

Stiffening her spine, Lynn turned to face him.

'I'll save you the trouble of sacking me. I resign. I didn't steal that pendant no matter where Ana says she found it. If you want to call the police I'll stay until they come, but I won't be back. I couldn't possibly continue to work in such a hostile environment. So if you will excuse me, I shall start my packing.'

'My office,' Luis snapped, totally ignoring everything she had said.

Grinding her teeth, Lynn followed him down the stairs and into the office where she paced the floor in front of his desk. With a face like a mask he observed her through narrowed eyes.

'Where will you go if I sack you?'

'Sack me? I resigned, remember.'

'No-one has accused you of stealing. Why should you assume I will want to call the police? I warned you at the beginning that my family were difficult people.'

Lynn stood still, dumbfounded.

'Difficult! Your relatives have just set me up as a thief and if I'm not to be charged, it is only because the Coenraads are such nice people.'

She was shaking with anger and plonked herself down in the chair opposite the desk. A heavy silence hung in the air as they scowled at one another.

'I asked you here to question you about the incident, no more. No-one is accusing you of anything. You are being hysterical. I don't believe for a moment that you stole Hella's pendant. What I hope to find out is how it was found in your room.'

Exasperated, Lynn sank deeper into the chair.

'I'm relieved to hear you say that but I am a nurse not a detective and I haven't the slightest idea how or why Ana found that pendant in my room, or even if she did,' Lynn added under her breath.

'You and Hella have been close this weekend. Could she not possibly have lost it, or left it in your room at one time?'

'No, senor, she could not. She was never in my room.'

He stretched back in the leather chair and, placing his long fingers tip to tip, pointed them beneath his lower lip.

'Now that matter is cleared up, I want you to come with me tomorrow.'

Lynn scowled at the sheer audacity of the man. How dare he dismiss Sofia's insinuation like that! He may be able to sweep it aside as of no more importance but she had her reputation to consider. What if she wanted other work on the island and her character was spoiled by these vindictive women?

'That won't be possible, I shall leave first

53

thing in the morning.'

'Tomorrow I must travel to see a valued colleague in the mountains. I would like you to come with me and on the way we will talk in more detail about how you might help me with my difficult family. Good-night, Lynn Raynor.'

Next morning, she had her cases packed and standing by her bedroom door as the clock on her bedside table showed seven o'clock. She was dressed in the same navy slacks with the turquoise top and navy jacket that she had travelled out in less than two months before, though now it seemed like a lifetime ago. Her nerves made her feel queasy or was it perhaps just hunger! She had stood by her bed for some time wondering whether to go down to breakfast or simply phone for a taxi from the hall and hope that no-one interrupted her.

She had sufficient money to stay in a hotel for the few days it would take her to book herself on a flight to England. Cross with herself for dithering like a schoolgirl, she straightened her shoulders and walked out on to the balcony, past the stairs and along the passageway guarded by the dark family portraits of long ago and went into breakfast. There was no-one about but Ana was busy at the table.

'I'm sorry. Am I too early?'

Lynn's voice echoed her distrust of Ana.

'No, no, the senor, he works in his office and my José, he helps Senor Peter. The guests are not yet up.'

Lynn was halfway through her light meal of orange juice and toast when Luis walked into the room. Her knife slid sideways off the plate, as her eyes surveyed his back from beneath her eyelashes as he helped himself from the sideboard.

'Good morning, Lynn. I hope you have changed your mind about staying with us.'

'I'm afraid not. I have a taxi calling in fifteen minutes.'

She wiped her lips with her napkin and made to rise as he sat down. 'Then you have fifteen minutes to spare me.'

His eyes locked with hers as Lynn sat back down in her chair and regarded him across the table. It had been a tremendous relief the previous evening to know that he believed her when she said she had not stolen the pendant, but she was still determined to leave.

It was time for her taxi and the air around the table had thickened to a point where it was difficult for Lynn to breath.

'Peter's cast is off. He has no need of me and I don't believe I can be of any use to either of the senoras.'

Without waiting for a response she stood up and left the room. When she had collected her luggage and made her way down to the courtyard Luis was waiting for her.

'I have cancelled your taxi. I need you to help me in the office. You need have no more contact with Sofia or Maria Medina than you wish. But I would be grateful if you will help keep Peter occupied until it is time for him to go to college. Meanwhile, meet me downstairs in the morning. If you are to help me, we have an early start.'

Would this man ever stop taking her breath away with his imperious bullying? How dare he send her taxi away, and what on earth did he think she knew about office work. She didn't want to go back to dismal London, of course she didn't, and now he had cleverly swept all her objections away by offering her a different job.

It would serve him right if she turned out to be hopeless in the office, she decided, as she turned slowly and returned her cases to her room.

CHAPTER EIGHT

The next morning was cloudy as Lynn, dressed in jeans and a warm blue sweater with a white top underneath in case it grew hotter later, made her way down the stairs to meet Luis. The blue Jaguar stood outside in the square as she came across the courtyard and through the cool hall.

Luis was waiting for her, dressed in immaculate linen slacks and a green shirt, the collar of which was open. He picked up a linen jacket from a nearby chair when he saw her enter the hall and swung it over his shoulder as he followed her out to the car.

'The damage was less than it looked,' he said, catching her furtive glance at the rear of the car and immediately acknowledging that he had known all along that she was the girl who had run into him outside the airport the day she had arrived on the island.

Lynn bent her head as he held the car door open for her. It was a very luxurious car, she admitted, as she fastened her seatbelt then watched Luis climb into the driving seat and start the engine.

'Teror is not so far away but it makes an interesting drive. My colleague, Carlos Alvarez, is terminally ill and can no longer work but he likes to be kept up to date with

57

our business affairs. His wife, Bianca, died two years ago of the same disease.'

Lynn frowned.

'I'm sorry to hear that.'

She felt his quick glance slide across her face and turned to gaze out of the window.

'Yes, it was a very sad time for him.'

They drove on in silence for several minutes. They had been heading back towards the city centre but now took a left-hand turning that took them away from the built-up area and into the mountains. The road was good but the farther they went, the higher they went and the twistier the road became.

The passing scenery was greener. Shrubs and trees collided across barren tracks of mountain side. White houses with red-tiled roofs clung to hillsides and gathered in green agricultural valleys beneath towering mountains fringed with pine forests.

'Maria Medina expects a lot from her niece,' he said suddenly, his voice breaking the silence of their journey. 'She calls it duty and I have never heard Sofia complain. But Enrique is a friend as well as my partner and I know he is very fond of Sofia. He would like to marry her but she has turned him down on several occasions.'

And we all know why that is, Lynn thought to herself.

'Sofia's mother was the sister of Maria Medina's husband's first wife so the

58

relationship between them is not strong. Yet they have lived together for ten years, ever since the death of my wife who was Maria Medina's only child.'

'How long has Sofia been a widow?'

'Sofia has been on her own for twelve years. Her husband was killed in a water-skiing accident six months after they were married. I never knew my father-in-law. He died not long after my wife was born. Perhaps what keeps the two women together is that they were both widowed early in their marriages. My wife was spoiled to a ridiculous degree but her way of life was strictly controlled nevertheless and it created a wilful, excitable, extravagant creature, much to her mother's disappointment. She was almost too beautiful with a fragile yet forged strength that burned the flame of life at an incredible rate. She died in a riding accident ten years ago. She was twenty-seven.'

Lynn watched his face as he talked, expecting to see a softening of his features as he referred to his wife. But his expression didn't change. If anything, it looked sterner than it had before and she felt a small flutter of fear for whoever loved this man.

'Sofia and my wife were great friends and it was perfectly natural that she took over the upbringing of my son when Mariana died. Peter's grandmother had already been diagnosed with heart trouble and we considered her not strong enough for the care of a boisterous seven-year-old.'

'And when Peter goes off to college, what then?' Lynn asked in a quiet voice.

'I am the only family they have. They will naturally stay where they are.'

When they entered the small market town of Teror the sun was burning off the remains of the mist that hung around the mountain tops. They left the car on a shady piece of ground on the edge of the old town and entered a neat, stone-flagged piazza with a lovely Moorish fountain in the centre. The home of Senor Alvarez was on the end of a terrace of houses that ran along one side of the square.

They were made welcome by father, daughter and grandson. Lynn, who had offered to sightsee rather than intrude, was made guest of honour as they plied her with polite questions and gave her advice on living here on the island.

It was in the warmth of this small, tragedy-stricken family that Lynn first saw the softer side of Luis Falcon. It was nothing short of a miracle. The taut lines disappeared from his face, flint grey eyes lost their stony indifference. His mouth softened and curved as six-year-old Vicente proudly presented him with a boat he had made. She couldn't drag her eyes away from this new aspect of her employer.

Later, Lynn was invited into the garden with

Vicente and his mother while Luis and Carlos talked business. Then they stayed for a light lunch after which they took their leave, Luis telling his friend that he wished to show Lynn around the town before they went back to Las Palmas.

Lynn was still in a cloud of euphoria as Luis led her back to the car after proving to be a wonderfully-informed and exciting guide. They had walked the streets of the old town with its white stone houses with pretty wooden balconies that had belonged to the nobles of the past. Luis had described the religious importance of the town and taken her to the Basilica De La Virgen Del Pino, the church of the virgin of the pines.

'In fourteen eighty one, it is said the Madonna appeared amongst the branches of the pine trees on this very spot and there has been a church here ever since. The one you see now was completed in seventeen sixty seven. The Madonna you will see inside is the Virgin of Gran Canaria and people come from all over the island on September the eighth to her festival. They walk for miles, sometimes falling to their knees and crawling through the town to the church to bring their gifts. It is a very emotional experience.'

He took her arm and led her into the church. Lynn was awed by the splendour of the magnificent Madonna whose jewel-encrusted gold adornments and altar dominated the interior of the church. A long line of people filed past continuously as Luis made his sign and bow before they both sat quietly and gazed at the shining spectacle.

Now, as she sat in the car next to him and listened to him promise to bring her to the festival in September if she was still here, her heart did a double switch and she knew without any doubt that she would stay.

Over the next few days, she found that the office work turned out to be less difficult than she had imagined. At first she was extremely slow on the word processor, taking over an hour on each letter Luis left her, but he never complained. Taking messages over the phone, sorting the important from the mundane, filing and filling in forms were second nature to her after her work as hospital ward sister and these she did well.

At the end of the first week her speed on the word processor was picking up and Luis had insisted she continue at the same rate of pay as she'd had before. She found that she was beginning to enjoy the work.

Luis was rarely in the office during the day and she had the place to herself. She kept well out of the way of the ladies and she had Peter if she got lonely.

On Friday afternoon, a week after she had started work in the office, Peter popped his head around the office door.

'I'm off out with friends today but if you're

not doing anything tomorrow I thought I might show you the rest of the island.'

She looked up from what she was doing.

'That would be lovely, Peter, thank you.'

He gave her a cheeky grin and disappeared.

Lynn smiled to herself and resumed her work. She now had both Saturdays and Sundays off and it would be nice to have Peter guide her to places she had yet to find.

CHAPTER NINE

The following day found Lynn and Peter out in the car Luis had made available for her. Peter was free of his cast now and in high spirits as they set off. They turned inland and Peter directed her to take a left fork up the narrow road to Bandama.

'It's a volcanic crater and we can only go along its rim for there is no way in or out unless you are a donkey. But a man lives down there alone. Then there is an eighteen-hole golf club at Atalaya on the other side of the volcano. Lots of famous people go there. Then we shall go to San Mateo and back over the mountains to Telde, where the cars race. It is very exciting there.'

The gradient had risen sharply with hairpin bends every few yards and nothing but sheer cliff face on both sides of the narrow road. Lynn made a face at the suspicious thought of the real reason for their day out. The last thing she needed after a drive like the one she was on now was an afternoon at a car rally. They arrived at the rim of the crater in one piece much to Lynn's relief and she pulled the car over on to the lookout platform and climbed out.

'It's fantastic,' she whispered approaching the fence and gazing down two hundred metres to the bottom of the crater.

'We are five hundred and seventy five metres above sea level here and over there is the golf course at Atalaya.'

He had come up behind her and was pointing over her shoulder.

'The crater was named after a Dutch wine merchant, Van Damme, who settled here in the seventeenth century.'

'How does the man down there survive on his own?'

'He will be mostly self-sufficient but when he needs to come out he will come up with his donkey. I think we should send grandmother down there to keep him company.'

They were both laughing as they climbed back into the car and Peter continued to guide her into the mountains. They had cheese and ham toasties and long, cool drinks of freshly-squeezed orange juice in San Mateo under the shade of a large umbrella as they gazed down the valley. Then they were on the move again through pine-clad mountains on tree-shadowed roads that wound around in a never-ending switchback.

It was from high up on the side of a narrow valley that Lynn first saw the house. It stood half hidden among the pine trees on the opposite side of the valley. She caught only a glimpse of it before they drove through a small village. For some reason she mentioned it to Peter and as they drove around the head of the valley and up the other side Peter suddenly pointed out an entrance on the roadside.

'I think that leads up to that house you saw,' he said.

Lynn pulled into the side of the road and parked the car. They couldn't see the house from the road but Lynn suggested they got out and took a walk up the unsurfaced track. Peter reluctantly agreed and they set off in search of the house.

'There are no fences or anything to say it's private. Do you think we are trespassing?' she asked.

'Fences are unnecessary here. All that is needed is a gate.'

He lifted his shoulders in a typical shrug.

'Well, there was no gate down there and this stony way can hardly be called a drive.'

After climbing for half a mile or so they came to a weed-shrouded clearing in front of the house.

'It's beautiful,' Lynn breathed.

'No, it is old,' Peter laughed.

Mist, like a wisp of silk, had vanished from the tips of the mountains, leaving a fresh silence alive with the sound of bird song and dripping water. The house stood high on the mountain side surrounded by the tall pines that hid it from the road below.

It was of Spanish design tempered with the Moorish influences of stylish archways and intricate pebble mosaics on the floor. A lone orange tree grew in the corner of the inner courtyard. Its branches, fruitless and overgrown, encroached beneath the roof tiles of the house.

A bang from above made them both jump as they turned from the dry fountain to gaze along the windows above the main entrance. The shuttered fronts of the windows were peeling, some hanging lopsided from broken hinges. The whole place had an air of distressed disintegration. From behind them an old man shuffled into the courtyard. His smile was welcoming as they turned their startled gaze towards him. Peter questioned him in Spanish. The old man replied and Peter translated it for Lynn.

'He is the caretaker.'

'Does he mind us being here?'

'Not at all, young lady. It is a long time since anyone took any interest in this house.'

The old man's English was slow and precise.

'My name is Manuel Carrara and I am delighted to meet you.'

'My name is Lynn Raynor and this is Peter Falcon. I am a nurse in the household of Peter's father. May we have a look around?'

'Please. If you want me I will be in the kitchen, through that archway,' he said, indicating the arched entrance at the back of the courtyard. 'Mind you, take care. The old house isn't as strong as it once was.'

Then he moved off across the courtyard and

they were alone once more.

'He was right about one thing,' Peter said, as Lynn moved towards a wooden staircase deep in the shadows of the lower gallery. 'We'd better be careful where we step. The whole place looks rotten to me.'

But Lynn was already in love with the house.

'Wait here for me if you're not interested. I must have a look around. I wonder how old it is and how long it's been empty. What kind of people lived here and where are they now? I mean, they must still own the place or why is the caretaker here.'

Peter followed her reluctantly up the stairs, dismissing her questions with a shrug of his shoulders. It was two hours before they sat down again on the edge of the dried-up fountain. The old man came out with two glasses of lemon drink on a tray.

'Have you seen all that you wish to see?' he asked.

'For the moment,' Lynn said, 'but I'd love to come again if I may.'

Manuel Carrara smiled.

'As often as you wish, senorita.'

Peter had finished his drink and was ready to go when the old man started to tell them a story in answer to Lynn's request to know the name of the owners of the house and why they didn't live there anymore.

'Fifty years ago, all this valley belonged to

one man. To enhance his fortune even more he married his only daughter to a colleague of his who was many years older than the girl. Their marriage was childless and in time she became bored and restless. Then one day she met a man and fell in love. They had an affair then her lover of several months, who was staying in the district but did not belong there, told her he must go home. He asked her to go with him but she refused.

'He was very angry and they parted on bad terms. Then one stormy night he returned to her house with a young girl, explaining she was a niece who had become pregnant and whose family had disowned her. He begged his lover to take the girl in. She could not refuse him and he vowed to come back in the spring and collect the girl and her child. But when he returned the house was locked up and the family gone.'

'What happened?'

'Who knows?' the old man replied.

'We must be going now, Lynn. Soon it will be too hot to sit here longer,' Peter interrupted.

'The young senor is right, senorita,' the old man said, as he rose to his feet and collected the glasses. 'I hope you will visit us again.'

He turned and made his way slowly back to the kitchen as Peter and Lynn hurried back to the car. The sun was directly overhead now and they had to wait several minutes for the interior of the car to cool down. Lynn followed the road down to Telde where again they stopped for drinks and a walk around.

'I suppose they could have found the girl a husband,' Peter said, as they strolled around after discovering there was to be no racing that day. 'And the senora's husband could have died and left her to marry again.'

'Then if her husband died, why didn't she wait until her lover came back and marry him?'

'We will never know, I suppose,' Peter remarked.

They were at the Hermitage of San Antonio when Lynn suddenly said, 'You know, I can't rid myself of the feeling that I have seen that house before.'

'Have you come this way before on your own?'

'No,' Lynn said, with a shake of her head.

'Then you have not. It must have been another house on some other island perhaps.'

'Perhaps,' she said, but she was unconvinced.

CHAPTER TEN

It was on their way back to Las Palmas, on the north bound motorway, that Peter suddenly broke the silence that had fallen between them.

'I shall tell them tonight.'

'Tell whom, what?'

The breeze from the open window blew Peter's hair back from his handsome face revealing his stubborn expression to Lynn as she slid him a sideways glance.

'The family. I shall tell them that I will study art and design in London. I will leave soon so that I have the summer to find somewhere to live and to be enrolled for the college. My cousin, Denys, writes and tells me what I have to do to accomplish this.'

'You have family in England?'

'Oh, yes, but my father does not communicate with them.'

'But surely you don't want to upset your father by going against his wishes. If he wants you to do a business course first he must have good reason. Wouldn't it be possible to do that, then, when he finds out you're not interested you could carry on with your art?'

'And waste several years, for what?'

Peter turned away and hung his hand out of the window.

71

'I have money of my own left to me by my mother. I can do as I will.'

Lynn sighed as she drove back to the Casa Mariana and garaged the car.

They were all gathered in the sala later that evening when Peter made his declaration. At first there was a deathly silence and Lynn held her breath. Senora Medina's cane rapped the floor.

'This disobedience will not be tolerated. It is obvious he is being exposed to outside influences.'

'Don't talk about me as though I were not here grandmother,' Peter said.

'How dare you speak to your grandmother like that!'

Sofia, her face frozen with shock, reprimanded him. Her ice cold tone continued.

'Your future is of great importance to the family. Your first concern should be that future as you very well know. It takes little insight to see where this other encouragement comes from,' she concluded and she glared across the room to where Lynn stood by the window.

'Enough, Sofia,' Luis said. 'Peter knows how we feel. If he is still determined to study art, then he's right. We can't stop him.'

'Well, if his own father cannot stop him I can and will,' Peter's grandmother declared. 'This money of his mother's he is so confident about can only be freed by my death or with my approval, and without money he can go nowhere.'

Peter's face paled with shock and Lynn's heart twisted on his behalf. A nerve jerked along Luis' jaw and he spoke sharply to the old woman, in Spanish.

'We are talking about Peter's wishes here. The money is irrelevant.'

There were strong emotions running beneath the surface as they all went into dinner that evening.

It was some surprise to Lynn when a few days later Peter arrived at her office door to say that his father had agreed to his plans and he would be off to England the following month. Lynn would be sorry to see him go and knew she would leave once he had gone.

She was a nurse not a secretary. Perhaps she should be looking for another nursing job here in Gran Canaria as she had first intended. She could try for an agency job with an independent flat. This live-in work was rarely successful.

Of course there was the comfortable accommodation which she would never be able to afford on a nurse's salary. The generous wages Luis paid her would be a hefty loss and then there was Luis himself. At the thought of never seeing him again her heart lay heavy and hard in the middle of her chest. She tried to examine her feelings for Luis and couldn't, he was such an enigma. Yet she had promised herself she would stay, at least until September and the Festival of the Virgin in Teror.

She had carried a chair out into the sunshine for her mid-morning break when she heard the Senora Medina calling for Peter.

'Peter,' her voice rang down from the balcony, 'come to me at once.'

For such a small woman her voice still held a strong authority.

'I'm afraid Peter isn't here, senora,' Lynn shouted back.

'Well, find someone else to help me down the stairs,' the old lady grumbled.

Lynn ran lightly to the stairs and looked up at the stiff figure waiting at the top.

'Where is everyone?' she demanded, before Lynn was halfway up.

'I'll help you,' Lynn said, coming to a stop two steps below the senora.

'I have no intention of allowing you to help me, Miss Raynor. Now, please remove yourself so that I may descend.'

Lynn tried to protest but was dismissed and had turned to retrace her steps down the stairs when the old lady's cane prodded her savagely in the back.

'Get a move on, girl.'

Lynn grabbed at the banister to stop herself falling, knocking aside the cane as she did so. There was a thump and shuffle behind her and

74

as she straightened up she was horrified to see the senora sliding down the stairs in an ungainly tumble.

Within minutes every member of the household appeared as if they had been waiting in the wings for their cue. With wild gestures and cries they clustered around the bottom of the stairs, blocking Lynn's path as she tried to stop them from lifting the senora before she'd had a chance to evaluate her injuries.

Moans came from the near transparent lips as Lynn felt for any broken bones. With relief she decided that she could detect none. Gently she took the quivering pulse then loosened the tiny buttons and opened the high collar of the senora's dress as her eyelids fluttered open. Sofia pulled Lynn away and fell on her knees by her aunt's side.

'Aunt, oh, Aunt, merciful heavens, what has she done to you? You've killed her,' she wailed when the senora's eyelids closed and lay still.

Then Luis was there, lifting Sofia to her feet, calming Ana and handing Sofia over to her before asking José to phone for the doctor. By the time the doctor came, the senora had been wrapped in a blanket and carried up to bed.

Lynn explained to the doctor and Luis what had happened and gave details of her actions, then she went to her own room, leaving the family and the doctor with the old lady.

Later that evening, Lynn went quietly along to check on her patient before going in to dinner. As she neared the sala she could hear voices raised in anger. They were speaking in Spanish but even so it wasn't hard for her to understand about whom they were talking for her name cropped up repeatedly.

There was a sudden silence as she entered the room. Enrique was standing next to Sofia whose immaculate make-up hadn't taken into account the natural flush of anger that stained it now. Peter was slouched in a chair beneath his father's pinning scowl. Luis turned from his son at her entrance and although there was no outward sign of anger, Lynn just knew he was furious.

'It would appear that no-one was around to witness this accident,' Luis said, waving a dismissive hand at Sofia who opened her mouth as though to speak, 'when Maria Medina fell.'

Enrique came over to Lynn and handed her a small brandy.

'For medicinal purposes, for you also must have suffered a shock.'

His smile was gentle, his large brown eyes warm with sympathy rather than blame. Lynn's muscles went slack with relief. She hadn't realised until then just how tense she was. Her mind was whirling with doubts. Had the senora really tried to push her downstairs, or had it simply been an accident? Although there was

76

no love lost between the two of them Lynn preferred to believe the latter.

'I insist she be sacked at once,' Sofia's steel hard voice demanded. 'You heard Aunt Maria tell you how it was. She pushed her when Aunt asked for help.'

Lynn gasped at the pure venom in the woman's voice. Enrique tried to silence her as Luis paced back and forth in front of the fireplace.

'It was an accident, pure and simple,' Lynn whispered.

She repeated her story omitting the part about being prodded by the senora's cane and ended by saying that because the senora was behind her she didn't know how she had come to fall.

'I'll see you in the office after dinner,' Luis said and Lynn stiffened her spine and threw out her chin.

She had nothing to blame herself for. If they were determined to make something out of this, then let them. She would pack up her bags and go as she should have done when her situation changed from nurse to secretary. She was a buffer to hang the blame on and her thoughts were all the more bitter because for a short while she had believed Luis Falcon when he had said he needed her help with his dreadful family.

But Sofia wasn't finished yet.

'Luis, get rid of her. She causes trouble for

77

everyone. She encourages Peter to go against your wishes. My aunt tries to hold him in check and she has this terrible thing happen to her. She knows the family has money. You have money, Luis, so don't fall for her scheming, sack her.'

'Sofia,' Enrique cried, and because it was so unexpected from such a quiet, unassuming person it drew everyone's attention, 'it is wrong to say these things.'

Luis' face was white with suppressed anger.

'Lynn was brought here with the express purpose of helping you and Ana with your duties with Maria. That she could also help keep Peter occupied during his recuperation was an added bonus. You, however, have rejected every offer of help from her and that is why she concentrated on helping Peter, whose ideas for his future, I might add, were made up by himself long before Lynn arrived.'

'I didn't ask for your help,' Sofia snarled. 'You didn't offer it all the years we were bringing up Peter. You never once showed concern then, but suddenly, when Peter is taking care of himself, I need help.'

Her mouth twisted and the ugliness that her beauty couldn't hide was displayed for all to see.

'Come, my dear, you need to rest. It has all been too much for you,' Enrique said, placing an arm around her shoulders and leading her away.

As they came towards the door where Lynn was standing Sofia turned to face her.

'Don't think your little tricks will work,' she hissed. 'I know where you are going, but Luis will never look at you. After my cousin, no woman can take her place in his life.'

The hatred that blazed in the other woman's eyes was out of all proportion to anything Lynn could have done or said and she was left at a loss to defend herself.

CHAPTER ELEVEN

After dinner, Lynn made her way to the office, determined to have it out with Luis once and for all. If he refused to believe her then she would be gone directly. There was no-one in when she arrived so she sat down to wait. Five minutes later he strode in and took her breath away with his first words.

'I wish to apologise for Sofia's attack upon you. You must realise that she, too, has had a terrible shock.'

'You believe me?' she asked.

'Of course.'

He smiled.

'I doubt very much that you would make a good murderer. It is an understandable accident although why no-one was with her to help her, I do not understand. Normally at that time of day she is lying down. Hopefully all will be cleared up in time.'

He seated himself on the corner of the desk and leaned forward to look into her face.

'And please, you must realise there is no reason for you to take this opportunity to make plans to leave again.'

Lynn was sure he would see her swallow. Her dry throat refused to contract.

'I . . . I had no such intention,' she lied.

'Good.'

He stood up and took her unresisting into his arms.

'I need you here, Rosalind Raynor.'

The kiss when it came was warm and firm, no hurried brush of the lips but strong and demanding like the man himself. Lynn answered it with all her heart until she felt her legs begin to give way and her lungs gasped for air. Then it was over and she leaned against his chest listening to the thrum of his heart echoing her own. Laughter barrelled up from his throat.

'If this is what it takes to keep you by my side then I shall enjoy being your gaoler.'

Lynn pulled away and looked up into his face.

'Are you making fun of me?'

Lynn was totally unprepared for this sudden show of passion and while she was delighted at his interest she was none-the-less wary of the reasons behind it.

On her way back to her room, she decided to call in on the senora again even though she knew the doctor had given the old lady a sleeping draught. It was on her way back out of the senora's bedroom after checking that she was still fast asleep that Lynn saw the painting.

She checked her step and turned back to look more closely. It was the house in the pines—the one she had visited with Peter! How strange that the senora should have a picture of that very same house, but now she knew where she'd seen it before.

Next morning she caught Peter making his way through to the kitchen with a large box of rubbish he had cleared out of his room.

'Peter, you remember the house we visited the other day? Well, there's a picture of that same house in your grandmother's room.'

'Great,' he said and disappeared with his burden into the back of the house.

Lynn ground her teeth and continued her way into the office. Of course it could simply be a coincidence. It did make a pretty picture, for in the frame was a much younger house—a lived-in house, with open shutters and flower bedecked balconies and water in the fountain.

Peter had reappeared in the doorway.

'Are you sure it is the same house?'

Lynn looked up from her work.

'Positive.'

'I will ask my grandmother. Ana says she is much better this morning.'

He marched off across the courtyard and Lynn smiled to herself for it seemed to her that Peter had grown into a man overnight. Perhaps it was the air of extra confidence he carried. Now he had faced up to his family and won.

He came back to the office just before lunch.

'Grandmother denies all knowledge of the house we saw in the mountains. She says the picture is no more than just a pretty picture.'

'Oh, well.' Lynn sighed. 'It was only a thought that perhaps she knew something about the people who had lived there.'

'I didn't believe her,' Peter stated.

Lynn was quite shocked to hear him speak of his grandmother like that. He had always seemed quite fond of her until their row the previous evening.

'Why don't you believe her?'

'I told her everything—how we found the old house and how we looked around it and met the caretaker, even told her the story he told us. At times, she looked as though she was going to tell me something, but then changed her mind. In the end she just said she didn't know what I was talking about.'

'But you think she did?'

'I know she was going to talk before she changed her mind. But what she was going to say . . .'

He spread his arms in a significant gesture.

When Ana came in with her coffee mid-morning Lynn asked after the patient and was told in a begrudging way that the senora, apart from severe and painful bruising, was recovering, with no thanks to you, she might as well have said by the look on her face.

When five o'clock arrived and Lynn was finished for the day she decided to take a walk. She had already visited most of the tourist attractions like the Santa Catalina Park and the sixteenth-century fortress of La Luz. She'd sunbathed on the soft white sands of Canteras beach and visited numerous museums, the house of Christopher Columbus and the Cathedral of Santa Ana. The list of things to see was endless but tonight she just wanted to walk, to amble through the old town and give herself time to think.

She was not homesick, far from it, although after a hot summer she thought with a smile she might even yearn for a spot of that cool English rain. No, she was convinced that she could live here quite happily for a long time. Finding somewhere she could be comfortable and do as she liked was the problem. She recognised the nesting syndrome, the need to gather and trim a place of her own.

She'd worked hard as a student, accepted help gracefully from older parents, and played the field in her early twenties but next year she would be thirty—the age Peter considered ancient—and life was moving on.

CHAPTER TWELVE

Lynn was on her way back through the narrow, cobbled streets of the old town when a small van drew up alongside her and a man leaned out of the window and called to her in Spanish. She signalled to him that she did not understand the language. He climbed out of the vehicle and came towards her, still speaking rapid Spanish.

Lynn glanced around for someone to interpret for them and noticed for the first time that the street was deserted. She turned to awalk way waving a hand at him to refrain him from following her. Then the man, shorter than herself but broad and dark, made a lunge and caught hold of her arm in a crushing grip.

The hand clamped tight over her mouth was broad and fleshy and she bit down hard on the base of his second finger. There was a stinging blow to the side of her head and all was blackness.

When she woke with an aching head and blurred vision her first recognition was that she was bound hand and foot by tight, sticky tape. As her vision cleared and she tried to move, a bolt of lightning sliced through her head. She became aware of a variety of aches and pains in various part of her body as she lay on her side on the floor of the van being bumped and jostled over rough ground.

Gradually her eyes became accustomed to the dark. The cab of the van was blocked off from the rear by a solid partition but there were two small windows in the back doors. Pale moonlight drifted through these to show her that the space around her was empty but for a large box behind the dividing partition. She wriggled painfully towards it without knowing why, simply following her instincts for survival. The box was locked. She fought the tears that trickled across her face and into her hair, and began to shuffle forward towards the back doors.

Once there, she lay still and gathered her thoughts. She could kick out one of the windows and try to get close enough to cut the bonds on her wrists. The window shot out on only the second kick but it flew out in one whole piece leaving no jagged edge to work on. Now what, she thought, chewing on her lower lip.

If only her hands were not behind her back. And how much time did she have before they reached wherever they were taking her? Her head spun with questions. What could they possibly want with her. Had they mistaken her for someone else?

In and out, round and round went ideas, hope and fear, until she was nearly sick. With a sudden rush of anger she lashed out at the doors with her feet. The doors burst open.

There was a rush of ground and a rattle of stones then she closed her eyes and rolled over the edge. The unsurfaced road robbed her of breath and bit painfully into her shoulder and hip when she hit the ground where she teetered on the edge of blackness once more. The warning of danger climbed up through the fog of pain and fear urging her into movement. She pushed herself with slow rolls into a ditch on the edge of a group of trees and lay still.

Hoping that the darkness would protect her, she allowed her eyes to close in an exhausted sleep. The stiffness had increased when she woke but she was still alone. Now she was aware of the trouble she was in. She must somehow find a tool to help free her from her bonds. Gently she began to feel around her immediate vicinity as far as she could reach.

There was nothing, then she remembered the window she'd kicked out. It must have shattered, but it would be at least a mile or two down the road. She had struggled to her knees before she was faced with the hopelessness of the task ahead of her. She couldn't hop a hundred yards let alone a mile, even if she could get to her feet.

She cried out as something dug into her leg and ripped her trousers as she tried to stand. Unable to get her hands down far enough to see what it was, she tipped backwards and the sharp instrument sliced into the bindings around her ankles. Carefully she pushed her ankles harder against the obstacle and there was a sticky, tearing sound as her legs came free.

With a gasp of relief she twisted her body and climbed to her feet. The moon was high now and she bent down to inspect the object that had torn her bonds. It was a sharp piece of tin. After judging as accurately as she could how it lay, she turned her back to it and bent down close to where she believed it to be. There was a sharp nick to her thumb as she guided her hands over it, then it sliced through the plastic, leaving a long tear on her arm. Now she was free, she mopped her battle scars and stared into the darkness around her.

The moon shone down on the hillside as Lynn, having no idea where she was, moved out from the cover of the trees. All around her, mountain tops were silhouetted against the skyline, sharp, jagged and barren. They pierced the night sky like the serrated edges of a gigantic knife.

It wasn't until she stumbled into a large, rough-edged rock and grazed her hands, that she saw the lights below her like twin needles along the valley floor. Was it the van? Were they looking for her? She crouched low behind the rock watching the lights grow as they bumped and twisted on to the mountainside and around sharp bends.

It was pointless to run. All she could do was

hide and hope they would pass her in the dark. Something ran over her foot in a flurry of dust and it took all her powers of self control not to scream. Afraid to look down she moved on, hurrying from shadow to shadow, trying as much as possible to stay out of the moonlight.

If she could reach the ridge ahead of her she would be safe. As the lights sliced over the bare terrain, Lynn dropped down behind the ridge with a groan of relief. She recognised the sound of the van's engine as it rattled by below. The lights disappeared into the distance and everywhere was plunged into silence. Now she was really alone.

*　　　*　　　*

Dawn was creeping up the mountainsides when Lynn caught the first signs of human habitation, a small square of whitewashed buildings with a rooster crowing from the top of a brokendown shed. With a rush of self pity she forced herself to hurry down the hillside towards the house.

The plump, middle-aged woman who answered Lynn's knocking filled the doorway.

'Si, senorita?'

'Please, will you help me? I'm lost.'

The woman frowned without understanding and spread her hands.

Lynn tried to mime her need, but still the

woman shook her head. Lynn was desperate when the man of the house came out to join his wife. Curiosity had brought him to the door and he had a little English.

'Help me.' Lynn pointed to herself. 'Help me get to Las Palmas, please. I,' she said, pointing to herself again, 'am lost.'

'Si, si,' he said. 'I help.'

He turned to his wife and together they entered the house, both speaking at the same time. Several minutes later he returned to lead Lynn gently into a battered truck where he helped her into the cab before climbing in. After two or three attempts, he started the engine.

Lynn bit down hard to stop herself from crying out as the truck bumped and jarred along the track. She had no idea how far away the city was and prayed that it wasn't too far. What she didn't expect was the truck pulling up after ten or fifteen minutes and the driver jumping out.

'I get help,' he told her.

Terrified that in some mysterious way the man she thought of as her rescuer was in fact in league with the men who had captured her gave her the energy to scramble out of the truck and stagger a few yards across the gravel.

Only when she lifted her head to look around her did she recognise her surroundings. She was standing in front of the house in the pines that she had visited with

Peter only days before.

They found her lying in a heap on the gravel only yards from the open door of the truck. Carefully, they lifted her up and carried her into the house.

CHAPTER THIRTEEN

It was well into the second day of her absence from the house of Luis Falcon that Lynn woke. She was lying in a small, four-poster bed with white cotton drapes tied back against the posts. A tall window shuttered at the bottom let in a ray of bright sunlight that bounced around the white walls to sparkle off the gold figure nailed to the wooden cross on the wall opposite the bed.

Lynn watched the small figure for a long time then closed her eyes and let out a long sigh. Manuel Carrara stepped into the room at that moment and caught her sigh.

'At last! We were worried about you.'

Lynn eased up on her elbow and smiled.

'How long have I been here?'

'Two days.'

'What?'

She lay back with a groan. Her headache had gone and the aches and pains in her body were much improved, but her stomach growled hungrily.

'I have made you something to eat now and Juanita will help make you comfortable.'

Juanita turned out to be the wife of the truck driver. She helped Lynn to an ancient bathroom then handed over Lynn's clothes all nicely washed and mended.

Lynn tried to thank her but Juanita only smiled and nodded.

When she was ready, Lynn left Juanita stripping the small bed and made her way down to the kitchen. Here Manuel was writing a note which he gave to Juanita's husband, Pedro.

He climbed stiffly to his feet as Lynn arrived and flapped his hand at the other man who immediately took his leave.

'I have sent word to your employer to let him know that you are safe. The truck broke down yesterday. Pedro worked on it all day but it will take time to find a new part so today he will walk to the village and ask Juan in the café to phone the Senor Falcon.'

Lynn smiled and thanked him and wondered what Luis had made of her absence. She ate the meal Manuel had prepared for her, then at his insistence sat in an old rattan chair under the balcony.

*   *   *

It was late in the afternoon when Luis, with Peter, arrived at the old house.

The old man welcomed them into the kitchen where wine, cheese and bread and a dish of olives were set out on the table. Lynn's heart skipped a beat when Luis' tall figure filled the doorway. She rose from her seat by the table to go to him when Peter rushed past

93

his father and crossed the room to her side.

'Where have you been? What happened to you? We have all been very worried about you. Father went to the police.'

He looked to his father for confirmation.

Luis broke off speaking to the old man to give a brisk nod towards Peter. Lynn felt what little colour she had leave her face at Peter's mention of the police.

'Oh, not the police.'

'There will be questions to answer most certainly,' Luis said, coming over to join them. 'How are you feeling, Lynn?'

'Well enough now, thank you, but I can tell the police very little.'

'Never mind, you can tell me all about it before we inform the police you are safe.'

'Come on, Lynn. We came up in Father's car. You'll be quite comfortable going back,' Peter encouraged, but Lynn was shaking her head. 'No, if Manuel doesn't mind, I'd rather tell it here.'

She sat back down in her chair.

'There is something about this place I don't understand. What, if anything, it has to do with what happened to me, I don't know.'

'I really don't think Senor Carrara . . .'

Lynn turned to the old man and smiled.

'Senor Carrara is a friend. Only he can help me tell this story.'

Luis' eyebrows drew down in a frown but he leaned back against a stone shelf to listen to what she had to say. Peter sat down at the table also and the old man let his hand cover Lynn's.

'There is a picture in Senora Medina's bedroom of this house as it was several years ago. Do you know anything about it?' she said, addressing her question to Luis who shook his head. 'Peter asked his grandmother about it but she denied all knowledge of it being the same house. She said the picture was just that, a picture. Yet Manuel will tell you that the picture in question was here in this house at one time.'

Lynn searched the faces around her, wondering what each one was thinking.

'What has this got to do with your disappearance?'

Luis' voice was sharp with suspicion.

'I'm not quite sure, but, please, bear with me. The last time Peter and I were here, Manuel told us a story about a love affair that went wrong.'

Here she hesitated, trying to find the right words to express her thoughts. Peter quickly related Manuel's story to his father.

Lynn waited until he had finished then continued with her account of what might be the truth.

'Could Senora Medina have been that young wife? If Peter's version was correct and the young niece was married off before the wife's lover returned after which she and her husband moved away, perhaps she was carrying her lover's child. In which case the senora would not want that knowledge made public.'

Luis' frown had become a darker scowl.

'You would disgrace my dead wife?' he said, with a voice that cut with diamond sharpness.

'I would disgrace no-one but somebody feared me enough to have me kidnapped two nights ago.'

One eyebrow rose, giving him a cynical expression.

'I doubt that. A more likely explanation is that you were picked up for a joy ride, or whatever they call it, by mistake, and being a reluctant participant were ejected from the vehicle and left to fend for yourself. That you were lost and wandered around all night I don't dispute, but kidnap? I think that might be a bit much for the police to believe.'

Lynn gulped back her disenchantment of her knight on a white charger coming to rescue her and whispered, 'If only you were right. Manuel made extensive enquiries but there was no mention of any niece being married off to a man in any village in these parts. So what happened to her? If the senora was the lady of this house and her husband died, why didn't she wait for her lover to return? We need your help, senor,' she said, feeling as though her heart was breaking for she did indeed love this man, no matter he should think the worst of her.

She related to them every minute of the horror of that night and how she had nearly given up before finding Pedro's and Juanita's house. She told them of the kindness and care she had received since coming into Manuel's home.

Manuel stood up and it seemed to Lynn as though he had grown straight then he started to speak.

'I am sorry that my story has caused so much trouble and I am pleased to have been of some help to the senorita in her need.'

He paused.

'I came to this house for the first time many years ago as a guest. Senor de Santos was a business associate of my father's. I resided at an uncle's house in the village. I saw her through an arch of water as the sun cast coloured sparks from it. I thought her to be the daughter of the house and determined to get to know her. My uncle and I had been invited for lunch and to talk business so it wasn't until I returned home with my uncle that I discovered that she was the wife of de Santos.

'Many times I watched her pass or sat at the table with them and each time my heart hardened a little more against a man of his years taking a girl half his age as a wife. In honesty, I was jealous. After a few weeks, my luck changed and my uncle and Senor de

97

Santos left on a business trip. I wooed and won the lady, unfairly I now know, but she was willing and we shared a beautiful summer. When it came time for me to leave, I asked her to come with me but she would not leave the comfort and security of her home. Our parting was bitter. I missed her dreadfully, but that was no excuse for what happened next.

'I became friendly with a serving girl and she fell pregnant with my child. Her family threw her out because she would not tell them who had done this thing. I was anxious that my father should not know so I took her to the one I truly loved, knowing that she still loved me and would not deny me help. I told her a story about the girl being a relative.

'If she believed me, I do not know, but she took the girl. When I returned as I had promised to do, the house was empty. I enquired then of the villagers what had happened but no-one knew anything. I have been here ever since.'

He hung his head as the silence in the room became uncomfortable. Luis was the first to break the silence.

'You say this woman's name was Santos,' he said to the old man, then turned an accusing glance at Lynn. 'My wife's name was Mariana Medina before we married.'

'Her mother's name,' the old man murmured.

'Sorry,' Lynn said. 'I don't understand.'

'Her name was Maria Isabella Medina de Santos. The women carry their mother's name with them into marriage,' Manuel replied.

'My mother-in-law's name is Maria Perez Medina,' Luis spoke quietly, 'and now I think we had all better go home.'

'Before you go, senor, I would like to show you something.'

They all trooped out of the kitchen after the old man and followed him across a moss-covered yard, through a gate and into an orchard. By the far wall they stopped and watched the old man drop to his knees. He moved to one side so they could see the wooden cross at the head of a grassy mound. Only the name Beatrix Sanchez was written there.

'Who was she?' Peter asked.

'The girl who carried my child.'

'Well, that clears that mystery up. She died,' Peter whispered.

But Luis and Lynn said nothing, just stared at the sad, little grave tucked at the back of an overgrown orchard.

CHAPTER FOURTEEN

Lynn's voice broke the silence inside the car as they made their way back to Las Palmas.

'She was buried in unconsecrated ground.'

'Without the blessing of a priest,' Luis added, a nerve pulsating at the corner of his jaw.

'What about the baby?' Peter queried from the back seat. 'Would they have buried it with her if it died?'

Lynn closed her eyes and wished she'd kept her mouth shut. She could feel the pain and anger emanating from the man at her side. That his family should be dragged into such an questionable past would be unthinkable to him. He was so proud and she loved him so much that she felt his pain as if it were her own even if she didn't quite see the situation as he did.

'I think we all know what Manuel Carrara was suggesting so we will leave the questions until we reach the house.'

His tone was so cold that it froze all the talk for the rest of the journey.

Once back at the Casa Mariana, Lynn hurried up to her room and lay down on the bed to think. If it was Maria Medina who had been Manuel's lover and her husband had died prior to the servant girl dying in childbirth say, then Maria could have fled with the baby and claimed it for her own. Much of the proof of this theory depended on dates and they would be easy enough to trace. But where did that leave the family, and what had been the point of her own kidnap attempt?

Lynn rose and took a shower as she tended the large bruises coming out all over her body. Some smaller ones were already turning a variety of colours. She dried herself with care, spreading antiseptic cream from her holiday medical bag along the cut on her arm, then she dressed for dinner choosing a long-sleeved blouse of light green. She wore it with a tan skirt of soft jersey material and placed gold stud earrings to match the thin gold watch on her wrist.

Luis was alone in the sala, the ladies not yet having put in an appearance and Peter was at friends for the evening, he informed her.

'Have you mentioned anything?' she asked.

'No,' he answered shortly.

'Then perhaps you would rather I didn't stay either. I could eat in my room.'

He swung his gaze to meet hers.

'You are as much involved in this affair as anyone and deserve some answers.'

'I know, but that could come later. I think my appearance would only antagonise your . . . the senoras.'

She saw him swallow a knot in his throat and longed to go to him and offer her comfort and understanding of how difficult the next hours were bound to be. If Maria Medina was guilty then she had done a foolish thing in keeping a child not her own. Even worse was to continue the deception after the death of Luis' wife.

At this point, the women entered the room and were offered drinks by Luis as Lynn took her seat by the window. He informed them of Lynn's lucky escape and of how she had been taken care of by a couple whose home she had come across in her wanderings. The police were searching for the culprits who had snatched her and they would then find out why they had done this dreadful thing.

The women glanced across to where Lynn was resting.

'She has come to no harm. Why should the police be interested? For all we know she went willingly,' Senora Medina said, tapping her cane on the floor.

Sofia, looking puzzled, shook her head.

'The people who gave her shelter told us a strange story about a family Santos who lived in the Casa Del Pino,' Luis continued, 'in the district of San Mateo.'

Sofia's face had paled considerably as she stared hard at Lynn.

'That was where Mariana was born and where you lived before your husband died, was it not, senora?' he addressed the old lady.

Without flinching she replied, 'That is

correct.'

'I know that Mariana was born in nineteen sixty-one but when did your husband die?'

'The same year and no, he did not live to see his daughter. We went to live in Tenerife at the home of my mother's family, which you know because you met my daughter there and brought her back here to live.'

They stared at each other and Lynn quaked at the intensity of their locked gaze.

'Senora,' Luis said in a cool, detached voice, 'we have reason to believe that my wife was not your legal child but the child of a servant girl left in your care when she became pregnant.'

Sofia's mouth had fallen open and a burst of indignation was directed straight at Luis.

'How can you say such things!'

The senora was neither pale nor beaten, her ramrod back as straight as ever and her stare as clear and direct. Lynn couldn't help but admire her for her indomitable spirit.

'I have never regretted it,' she said in a clear voice. 'The child had no future without me and I had no chance of a child for myself, for I had no intention of marrying again. My husband died of a heart attack while on business in Tenerife and I had him buried there. I was too ill to go to his funeral and a week later the baby was born. There was no time for a doctor and the only two servants in the house were well paid to keep quiet after the girl's death.

They buried her in the orchard. Anything else would have spoiled my plans.'

She ignored the horrified look on her niece's face and gave her full attention to Luis.

'What about Lynn's abduction? That was your doing also was it not and why?' he demanded.

'She was always a nuisance, poking her nose into matters that did not concern her. I thought to frighten her only. She should have had the sense to leave this house and find another job,' the senora snapped. 'You and Sofia were a perfect couple. After all that she has done for you over the years, you should have made her your wife. You owed it to her.'

She shook her cane at him.

'But, no, you must make eyes at this stupid, insipid English miss. Your behaviour is on an equal only with your son. But then,' she said, her beady eyes landing on Lynn, 'like will find like. You are neither of you of the old blood.'

With that she signalled Sofia to help her rise and together they left the room.

The silence stretched like elastic and only snapped them back to the present when José arrived to announce dinner. Ana did this job as a rule and Lynn did not miss the telling look on José's face as he retreated quietly. Luis let it go and together they went in for their meal.

Luis tried to make polite conversation during the meal and Lynn participated to the best of her ability but there was an

104

awkwardness between them that had never been there before. Oh, there had been coldness, fury, resentment and a multitude of other emotions but never had Lynn felt the inability to help so strongly.

'We will take coffee in the office,' Luis stated at the end of the meal.

Lynn half smiled at his presumption but preceded him down the stairs and across the courtyard to the office where José was setting out the coffee. Luis told him to leave them and after the door had closed behind the old man he turned back to the desk and served Lynn with her coffee.

Then, taking his own cup, he moved around the desk to sit in his normal seat. The grim lines on his face gradually eased as he stared at her over the top of his cup.

'You have a surprising ability to trail trouble behind you. First you try to drive over my car, then you risk your life to rescue my son. I have to bribe you to get you to come and take up what I think of as a perfectly normal position and before I can turn around you have encouraged my son to make a stand for himself, and made an enemy of the people I employed you to help. When I think I have found the solution to that problem, you get yourself kidnapped and nearly killed yet again. This time your revelations have far-reaching consequences.'

He placed the cup back in the saucer and,

steepling his fingers, raised them to support his chin. Lynn watched him like a hypnotised rabbit. Her heart thumped at twice its speed and her stomach felt so queasy it was an actual pain that would have bent her over had she been standing.

None of this showed on her face she was sure as she said, 'None of it was my fault.'

He smiled and Lynn was sure she was going to die.

'What will you do now you know the truth?' she asked.

'What do you think I should do?'

Lynn moved around restlessly in her chair. She was too old for this sort of thing.

'Well, do I start looking for a new job?'

'You see, there you go again, threatening to run away when I need you most.'

She caught the glint of humour in the depth of his eyes and realised she was being teased. She couldn't believe it, then she remembered how he had laughed while visiting the Alveras family in Teror and how it was then that she first realised that she loved him. Indignation flooded her face. How dare he tease her when there was so many questions still unanswered? He was cruel—why else would he play with her feelings like this?

Before she knew what she intended, she had jumped to her feet and hurried across to the door. His voice halted her as her hand clenched the handle.

'Nothing has changed. Peter will go to England in three weeks' time as planned. Enrique will waste no time in marrying Sofia now she has at last agreed to his proposal.'

'Enrique and Sofia are to marry?'

'They are. They will live here with the Senora Santos. We will keep the ground floor for business purposes.'

His intent gaze was unsettling her.

'I don't understand,' she said with a frown. 'We'll stay as we are?'

'No, we are not to live here. You may go back to your nursing if you wish, with a glowing reference.'

His words hung in the air like a guillotine while time left her lips on a breath and was gone.

'You are giving me notice, from when?'

'I have another proposition to put to you,' he said. 'If I was considering marriage, a new wife would not be happy to share her home with family, legal or otherwise.'

'True,' she whispered, seeing her dreams of love between them drifting out of reach.

'I would have to find a wife first, of course.'

'Of course.'

'Then I would have to find a home for us.'

'You would.'

'I would like you to look at these plans,' he went on and he handed over a wad of papers.

She looked down at the sheets spread out on the desk top.

'They're proposals for the modernisation of an older property,' she murmured, puzzled as to what this had to do with a job proposition for herself.

'We have two or three weeks yet before Peter leaves. Sofia's marriage will take place shortly after that. While this is happening the builders will be doing structural repairs on the house, and I will still need you here. Afterwards I will be going away on business for several weeks. During that time I would like you to continue helping Enrique in the office here then to oversee the finishing work on the house.'

Lynn's jaw dropped. Not only was she being ejected from his love but he wanted her to fit out his house for some future bride. Words failed her.

*   *   *

Lynn looked up from the postcard she had received that morning from Peter. It was the picture of Big Ben and an enthusiastic message that read, I am loving London and my flat mates are good guys. All around me I find the inspiration I need. Soon I will be very famous and the family will be proud of me. Peter.

They were still his family, she mused.

Sofia and Enrique were married and apart from them moving into Luis' larger room, very little had changed. She had given up her room on the first floor, despite Enrique's protestations and moved into a small guest room beside Luis' office.

Tomorrow Enrique was to drive her up to the village of Santa Lucia where she would stay in a small hotel while she saw to the renovation of Luis' new house. The days were getting longer and hotter as spring gave way to summer. The air conditioning in the small car was working in top gear as Enrique manoeuvred them around the mountain roads.

'I'm sure I was up this way with Peter the day we found . . .'

Here she stopped because she couldn't bear to think of the Casa Del Pino and the dreams the house had awakened in her.

The hotel was tiny, simply furnished and spotlessly clean. Lynn said goodbye to Enrique after being given directions and instructions for her new job. The builders would still be there finishing off interior work and she was to make use of them for anything she felt still needed attending to. All in all Luis had given her a free rein.

Her heart lightened that afternoon as she started out to find Luis' new house. It was a nice day. She had an easy job, and was looking forward to the challenge. Enrique had arranged a lift back to Las Palmas with a friend from the hotel.

As she turned at the head of the valley and

accelerated up the pine-sheltered road she knew without doubt where she was going.

The house burst into view as she left the cover of the pine trees and drew to a halt on the gravelled forecourt. Tears blinded her to Pedro's old truck and a large white van with lettering in blue scroll along the side. As she stepped out of the car she could hear voices and banging.

How cruel of him, she thought, to send her here. She shook off her sadness and entered the hall. Manuel was the first to see her. His smile was beautiful as he took her hand and led her into the inner courtyard.

'Senorita, welcome.'

The shutters and old floorboards had been replaced and the windows shone in the late afternoon sun. Everywhere weeds and moss had been scraped away. New tiles replaced the old ones uprooted by the overgrown orange tree, now pruned and neat. The smell of varnish hung like a cloud in the hot air.

It was all as she had pictured it, as Manuel had described it in its earlier days, right down to the crystal images through the fountain's spray. In another world she wondered dreamily, did Manuel see the image, too?

Suddenly, Luis stepped out from behind the spray. Manuel had vanished. Suddenly, it all became clear. Luis had arranged all this for her. She was not alone in her feelings that love had flourished between them. They were to live here, in the house among the pines.

'You promised to take me to the Madonna's fiesta,' she said, locking her gaze with his.

She could see her image reflected in his eyes and her heart bounded with hope as he leaned forward and placed his mouth to hers. Then she was pulled closer and held firmly in his arms as the kiss deepened.

'I was so angry with the spitfire who bumped my car yet I could not drive off and leave her. I followed her all the way into Playa. Why did I do that?' he asked when at last they separated.

Still dazed Lynn shook her head. Then she was being enfolded in his arms once more.

'When you rescued Peter it was as though fate was speaking to me. I had to have you near me.'

Lynn nodded, her head against his chest.

'You are the flame to my hearth, the food for my heart and the air for my breath. You will marry me and stay by my side for ever. Say you love me, my dearest Lynn.'

It was not a question but a statement of fact and Lynn, hiding a secret smile, heard the faintest quiver of uncertainty in his demand.

'With all my heart,' she answered, raising her face to his.